THE EVIL
HAS LANDED

By Robert N. Going

Where or When Lyrics by Lorenz Hart, Music by
Richard Rodgers, Copyright © 1937 Williamson Music

Once Upon a Time Lyrics by Lee Adams, Music by
Charles Strouse, Copyright © 1962 Charles Strouse and
Lee Adams

Although inspired in part by actual events, this book is a
work of fiction. Names, characters, places and incidents
either are products of the author's imagination or are
used fictitiously. Any resemblance to actual events or
locales or persons, living or dead, is entirely
coincidental.

First Edition

7/17/08

To Aunt Joanne,

Because I'm pretty sure
you'll read this before
he does!

Rob

For Pudsey,
who makes all things possible.

Prologue

July.

And there she stood, just as he knew he would find her, firmly rooted at land's end, her green eyes gazing out to sea and the darkening horizon, the ocean breeze caressing her blond hair, the softness of her face misted by the crashing surf far below. In another time some master craftsman would have seized the moment and carved her haunting likeness for the prow of some Nantucket whaler, destined to enchant forever distant waters and storied lands.

He paused before approaching her, drinking in the vision. Barely eighteen years old and she was already . . . what? A flight of fancy? The stuff that dreams are made of? He smiled at the thought. Something like that.

She was . . . poetry.

Not like the others, not like one of those free-verse floozies his mother had warned him about. No, this one had structure and purpose and permanence, and strictly metered lines, so to speak.

He turned a verse over in his head:

> *A touch of gold, a glimmer in her eye,*
> *That ancient pagan hordes could never hold*
> *Is mine till dust.*

He sighed.

But enough of this worshiping from afar crap.

"Hey, stranger!" she greeted him warmly.

"Strange, perhaps, but hardly stranger. Graduation was, when? A short month ago?"

"A lifetime. Don't you feel it, feel how different everything is now?"

He cleared his throat. 'Yeah, well different doesn't sound so bad to me. I can't wait to get the hell out of here."

"Oh, come on!" she laughed merrily. "High school wasn't that bad."

"For you, maybe. Everyone likes you."

She patted him on the arm. "People like you, too. They really do."

"Yeah, well maybe when I'm dead someone will mention it." He paused and then looked at her, really looked at her. "Can I tell you something?"

"Sure!" she said.

"I'd like to pay you a compliment."

"Go right ahead!" she giggled.

"I'd like to pay you the biggest compliment anybody ever paid anybody."

"Go for it!"

"I just want you to know," he began slowly, "that knowing someone like you exists, knowing *you* exist," and here he paused briefly as he had practiced, "makes life almost *bearable* for me."

He waited.

"That is SO SWEET," and she kissed him on the cheek, the first time any girl ever had.

Not exactly first base, but at least he was in the game.

Thank God she wasn't like the others, snooty little monsters with their wicked little amusements, toying with human emotions, ripping your guts out for sport. This one had always been different. Kind. Never done or said those things which some girls do to show their . . . displeasure. She had always treated him exactly the way she had treated everyone else, and that was pretty damn . . .NICE.

There was no stopping him now. He was on a roll.

"You are really, truly, the nicest person I have ever met."

And she touched his arm again, this time letting her fingertips linger.

He plowed ahead.

"You are a delight. An absolute delight. A most precious thing."

And now she tilted her head to his shoulder in an "aw, shucks" sort of way before modestly stepping back.

"So anyway, before we go our separate ways down life's cruel path," he extemporized, for he really hadn't planned anything this stupid, "I just want you to know how much I love you."

She froze.

And he felt her freeze, even though he was looking at his own shuffling feet.

Then he froze, too. And stuttered and mumbled and back-tracked and muttered and explained, "I mean, you know, like a FRIEND, right? I, I, I didn't mean anything more than that."

Her head bobbed in mock disbelief as she looked right at him and those eyes burst into a devilish glint.

She smirked.22

She SMIRKED!
Then, she must have seen the rage.
"I think you'd better leave."
"Not yet," he said.
"Cut it out. I'm going home."
 His life's story caught up with him.
"Yes. So long."

As she sailed through the air to the rocks below, he thought he heard her scream. But if so, that pretty little scream was soon swallowed up in the wind and the battering waves, crashing, crashing, crashing in steady metered rhythm.

When a suitable period of time had passed and he was convinced she would breathe no more, he called the police. It took several hours for the rescue team to recover her body.

He wept publicly for his classmate and shouted that it was all his fault, that he should never have taken her so close to the edge, that he should have known about the dangerous wind currents that could knock you off your balance so easily. Friends, neighbors, strangers, all tried to comfort him. All could plainly see how much he had loved her. Finally his mother arrived and took him home where he spent the night in somewhat fitful sleep.

The next day was sunny and warm.

And two men walked on the surface of the moon.

Chapter 1.

Ft. McBain, NY
Palm Sunday, 1999, 0400

Jack Hughes had seen blood before, cuts and gashes and a couple of fairly serious motor vehicle accidents, but nothing had prepared him for this: the liquid life of one human being spread over two flights of stairs, three hallways and three rooms of the apartment where the stabbing took place. Remarkably the EMT's had found signs of life and the eccentric young woman who lived alone survived another half hour before expiring under the harsh lights of the hospital emergency room.

The 33 year old Assistant District Attorney had just completed his first year on the job in the small county where there were a grand total of two part-time ADA's, assigned routinely to negotiating traffic tickets and prosecuting minor offenses. The felonies were the nearly exclusive domain of the District Attorney himself. Not tonight, though. Mr. District Attorney had unplugged his phone after being interrupted three times the night before by third-shift rookies looking for guidance on filling out appearance tickets; the senior ADA was out of town, and Jack wasn't.

Knowing he had the blessing of the Sheriff, Jack enjoyed the freedom of the road driving the 22 miles to Fort McBain. He knew the location well, a block behind the small police station, the apartment building attached to the dingy neighborhood grocery store where Jack occasionally purchased a Peach Snapple under the suspicious glare of the neighborhood hangers-on. Sheriff Emory Rushmore met him in the gravel parking lot across the street. It was three hours before dawn and the pop flashes of the police camera from the otherwise dark third floor windows cast an eerie specter over the scene.

" What we have here is a homicide. The victim lived on the third floor. She was found just inside the front door in the ground floor foyer."

Foyer seemed like such an elegant word for a narrow dark hallway leading to the steep staircase lit only by a raw bulb on the second floor landing.

" She was found there by two of her neighbors, allegedly. They claim they tried to get in the building but had to push the door open because the victim was lying behind it. Given the cast of characters, let us say I am a bit reluctant to accept their stories."

" And the names are?" Jack inquired.

" The victim is Patty Hartwick. The neighbors who found her are Daisy Nichols and Martin Kilhooey."

Round up the usual suspects. No strangers here.

Daisy had called the ambulance, she said. Then, she said, she rode with Patty to the Littleburgh Hospital. Patty died in the ER without regaining consciousness.

" Let's take a look at the scene," Jack suggested. One look at the blood made him less sure that this was such a hot idea. Remarkably, though, he was not one tenth as grossed out by the discharges of the Fountain of Life as he was by the globs left by the collisions of jars of strawberry jam and mayonnaise outside Patty Hartwick's apartment door, generously merged with each other and a small pool of blood. At the time he didn't notice a portion of this mess lodging on the point of his wing-tipped shoe. After this day he would never wear them again.

He passed into the kitchen, where a small bloody footprint stared up from the worn linoleum. The tiny bathroom had a red-stained bra and blouse soaking in the sink. The living room (or in this case, the "dying room") was lit only by the glow of the portable television, still on, with only late-night static. No cable tv in these digs.

The lounge chair was blood soaked and draped over it an old sleeping bag with numerous sharp tears. Stabbed watching tv. Was she even awake? Jack's flashlight caught a glint under the television stand. A piece of a broken beer bottle. He soon found the other pieces at the base of the wall behind the television. Quickly shooting the beam up the wall he detected long liquid streaks. So she HAD been awake, enough to hurl her bottle of Piels at her attacker. Or maybe she just hadn't liked *Saturday Night Live* that night.

"Well, let's start with the obvious question," said Jack to Sherwood Gray, the sole Fort McBain village policeman on duty. " Who sleeps with whom among this cast of characters?"

Gray laughed. "In this end of the village, everybody sleeps with everybody."

"Including Patty and Daisy?"

"Everybody."

He turned to the Sheriff. "Where's Daisy now?"

"We've secured her in a room at the P.D. with a matron watching her. I've instructed the undersheriff to assign an investigator to talk to her."

"Why doesn't the undersheriff interview her himself?"

Rushmore laughed. "Young man, in time you will learn the answer to that question. Meanwhile, let's take a closer look around the rest of this place."

Undersheriff Whelan Oates grimaced. He had been given the unpleasant task of assigning an investigator to interview the suspect, and he knew that Bull Heimlich was not only the first one on call, but also the best man for the job. And he hated Bull Heimlich.

Oates and Heimlich had joined the Sheriff's Department about the same time. Oates was a go along, get along, do-what-you're-told type who steadily rose through the ranks, accomplishing quite little in the process, but not messing up a whole lot. Heimlich, in contrast, was an in-your-face, seat-of-his-pants high flyer who generally achieved what he set out to do, but in a manner that often gave his superiors heartburn and caused District Attorneys to wince. He was particularly effective in interviewing women, and his legendary "Heimlich Maneuver" with the ladies created some jealous hostility, but mostly grudging admiration among his co-workers. The not-nearly-so-successful Oates was among the former. In fact, Oates had been so unsuccessful in that field that he had managed to convince himself that he possessed a superior moral code.

"Bull, this is a serious murder case and I don't want you screwing it up," Oates lectured. "This is almost certainly going to trial and I don't want the evidence tainted by any unorthodox methods. Understood?"

"Sure," said Bull. "In other words, you just want me to do what I always do."

Oates seethed. "Let me make myself clear. There will be no Heimlich Maneuver used on this suspect!"

Bull stood up. "Whatever you say, boss. But you know, " he whispered as he leaned across the desk, "I'd rather use the Heimlich Maneuver than that hiney-lick maneuver that you used to get this job." He turned to leave.

Oates sputtered, but he couldn't think of a thing to say. Not one thing. Halfway through the door, Bull turned and said, "Whelan, can I ask you a personal question?"

"I guess."

"When your parents got married, did all the guests sit on the same side of the church?"

Oates looked puzzled. "Well, how would I know that? I wasn't there."

And as the door closed and Oates heard the gales of laughter on the other side, after a long pause, the mist lifted.

"That son-of-a-bitch. That goddam son-of-a-bitch," he muttered.

~

"Hi, Daisy. Howya doin' today?" Bull asked casually as he strolled into the interview room. He made direct eye contact and was careful to remove all trace of a leer from his natural smile.

Daisy Nichols was rough-looking, thin of the malnourished type, grubby jeans with tattered jean jacket, scraggy hair, a face only a mother could love, and then only if the mother had been as drunk as Daisy's had been before the Social Workers had finally removed her from the home when Daisy was seven. It was difficult to observe the contours of her body, but Bull, who was generally not particularly fussy in that regard, was convinced that it was of the type that only attracted close relatives and stepfathers. Her rap sheet said she was 29. That she was over the age of sixteen without at least three illegitimate children classified her as an Old Maid in Fort McBain.

He settled in across from her. "So what's the story, Daisy? What happened to your friend?"

"Well, it's like I told the Sheriff. I come home around one o'clock this morning and I can't get the front door open, something was blocking it, so I get Martin and I go, 'Hey, something's blocking the door. Help me get in', so he goes, 'sure' and we push on the door and it was her, Patty, and she's just laying there covered with blood, and I go, 'Martin, I'm gonna call an ambulance' and I did."

Bull smiled, remembering his perfectly-grammared mother correcting him: "In this house, we go, 'SAID'!"

"And you rode with her in the ambulance?"

"Right."

"And then she died."

"Right."

"Well, I guess that about covers everything," Bull said. Is it ok if I type up a statement for our records?"

"Sure,' she said. "Why not?" looking very relieved.

Bull inserted a standard statement form into the typewriter. Word processors were not in the budget yet of the Fort McBain Police Department, and as the Sheriff's Office had only had them for a couple of years, he was an old-pro with this antique electric.

"I'm a pretty good 'hunt and peck' typist," he told her. "Some guys are more hunter than pecker. Me, I'm definitely more pecker than hunter."

"That's what I heard about you," she laughed. "They say Bull Heimlich's all pecker."

"You heard right." Remembering his orders, he said no more on that subject.

"Now, " he said officially, "the first part of this form says that you've been advised of your rights, including the right to remain silent, the fact that anything you say can be used against you, that you have the right to an attorney; if you can't afford one, one can be provided for you without cost. Do you understand these rights?"

"Yeah, I know my Remander rights," she frowned, "but why am I getting those? Am I a suspect?"

He smirked familiarly at her, "Why, should you be?"

"No. I didn't do nothing."

"All right, then. Let's get on with it so I can take my kids to church. They're giving away palms today."

She laughed and he laughed with her.

Sheriff Rushmore sat in Carl Brown's living room with Carl, his sons Carl, Jr. and Andy, Andy's girlfriend Christy Martini, Carl's mother Marge Brown and Eleanor Glaskey, a tenant in the apartment next to Daisy's. The younger ones were pretty upset, the girlfriend particularly. The Sheriff pieced together what had happened as they saw it.

Around 9:00 p.m. on Saturday Daisy Nichols and Martin Kilhooey were hanging around Larry's Market drinking beer and shooting darts. Marge was tending the store.

"Why is it called 'Larry's'?" The Sheriff interrupted.
They all looked at each other, then back at the Sheriff and shrugged.

Patty Hartwick came downstairs from her apartment and bought a couple of six-packs of Piels beer. Daisy started in with her.

"Why'd you quit your job? Whadya gonna do now?"

"Beats me. I don't care. Hated the job."

Daisy was getting agitated. "I got you that job. Then you go and quit, you stupid bitch?"

Patty walked out without saying another word. Daisy sucked down another brew.

"Don't worry about her," said Marge. "She got her refund this week, so she's got a few bucks. Why don't you two go upstairs and play cards or something. I've gotta close up."

Daisy and Martin left the store and went upstairs in the attached apartment building.

About 1:35 a.m. Andy and Christy arrived at the Brown apartment. The door was locked so they waited in the car for a few minutes until Carl, Jr. and their cousin Steve Draybach came back from the pizza place five minutes or so later. They had hardly sat down when there was a knock at the door. Daisy Nichols.

"There's something blocking the front door to my apartment. Could you guys help me get the door open?" So they all trooped off next door and the boys were able to shove it open enough to get in. And wish they hadn't.

Patty Hartwick lay sprawled head first down the last three steps with her body lodged against the door. A trail of blood followed behind her as far as the eye could see in the dim light. Andy ran next door with Christy to call an ambulance. Cousin Steve waited in the street to flag down the ambulance. Daisy stayed off to the side. Carl Jr. heard moaning and knew Patty was alive. He leaned close to her and asked what happened. "I don't know," he heard and she settled back into soft incoherence. Andy and Christy rushed back.

"They said to keep her head up," he cried and the boys picked up the near lifeless body and carried her a short distance to the front steps. Christy cradled the dying woman's head in her lap while Daisy just stood. It was cold for late March, light flurries in the air.

"Somebody get a blanket," said Christy. "We need to cover her and keep her warm."

"No!" said Daisy, off to the side. "Get a white sheet. Cover her with a sheet."

So Andy raced up the stairs past the pools and swaths of blood, up, up to the third floor, over the mayonnaise and the strawberry jam and the broken glass, past the broken doorknob and through the open door, stopped for just a moment in horror at the sight of the blood in the kitchen, held his insides together long enough to grab a sheet off the bed and raced back down, tossed the sheet to his brother, kept going and puked his guts out in the alley between the buildings.

When he was finished he looked up and saw Martin Kilhooey walking stiffly up the alley, a boot on one foot, a bread bag on the other, a brace on the bagged leg.

"What the hell happened to you?"

"Surgery yesterday on the knee."

Martin told him that he had come home from a walk same time as Daisy and they couldn't get in, so he had gone around the back to see if he could climb up on the flat roof over the store and get in the building that way, but with his leg he just couldn't do it. Andy told him quickly about Patty and helped him hobble out to the front just as the ambulance arrived.

The ambulance crew worked efficiently as Daisy stood and watched. The driver noticed her and said, "Do you know who this is?" When Daisy affirmed he said, "Come with us to the hospital, then. We'll get the information we need as we go along."

So Daisy hopped in the ambulance, tried to go in the back with Patty, but all three members of the crew told her to stay up front.

Marge picked up the story from there.

After the ambulance crossed the bridge over the river about a half mile from the apartment, Daisy suddenly jumped out of the moving vehicle as it slowed for a red light. She ran the several hundred yards to Marge's house. It was nearly two a.m. when she heard her doorbell ring.

"This had better be good," she said as she saw Daisy on her porch.

"Patty's hurt real bad, real bad. I think she might have attempted suicide. We've got to go to the hospital. Your grandkids are real upset."

So Marge threw on some clothes and they drove back to the apartment. After comforting the teenagers, assuring them that their father should be getting home soon, as the bars were closing, she took Daisy and Martin in her car and drove to the Littleburgh Hospital. When they got there, the hospital people were still working on Patty. Daisy tried to approach, but the Doctor told her firmly to please wait in the lobby.

The ambulance driver was still there, and Marge observed from a distance that he looked a little angry, came over and said something to Daisy and handed her a piece of paper and a pen. Daisy wrote something and handed it to him. Then she quickly left the hospital and waited in the car. After a few minutes the nurse told Marge that Patty was dead.

"This was NOT a suicide, Mrs. Brown!" she stated rather emphatically. Shortly after, Marge and Martin joined Daisy in the car.

"What'd they want from you?" Martin asked her.

"My name and address. I wrote down that I was Polly Eckler from Canal Street in Sanford Mills."

"What the hell did you do that for?" Marge demanded in her stern, motherly voice.

"I have my reasons," she replied quietly. "They better not try to pin this on me. I have an alibi. I was at your daughter's house."

"I don't believe it. What were you doing at Marie's house at that hour?"

"She was babysitting Eleanor's daughter, so I knew she'd be up. Just went over to talk." Daisy looked down and said nothing more on the twelve mile trip back to Fort McBain.

They arrived back to the Brown apartment. Carl, Sr. was home now, cousin Steve had left, and Eleanor Glaskey, having arrived home to find her

-11-

building secured by the police, and having been advised politely that it was unlikely she could have access to her apartment before noon, had joined the group, her options being somewhat limited.

Christy was still sobbing. Daisy went right over to her and started stroking her hair. "I'm so sorry for what happened to your friend," she told Daisy, as Daisy continued to pet and coo and hug her. Just then Marge, who had lagged behind a little to check with the police, walked through the door.

"Get your hands off of her," she warned Daisy with ice in her voice. Daisy backed off without a word.

A few minutes later Sheriff Rushmore knocked on the door, asked to see Daisy, and took her over to the police station around the corner for questioning. Another Deputy came for Martin a few minutes later.

And that, Sheriff, was all that happened till you came back here now.

"Excuse me a moment, Daisy," Bull apologized with disgust. "Looks like I'm getting bothered again." He was responding to Jack Hughes' knock on the door.

Once the door closed behind him, Bull greeted his friend. "What's up, old buddy?"

"She go for it yet?"

"Nah, we're just getting started. You know anything?"

Jack filled him in on what the Sheriff had learned.

"I like the part about the sheet."

Jack agreed. "Adds a touch of the *macabre*, don't you think?"   "I'll say. Wanna sit in for a while?"

"Sure."

"Daisy, this is Jack Hughes. He's an assistant district attorney, big hotshot law-yer from Sanford Mills, and he's gonna sit in here to make sure I don't do anything nasty, ok?"

"I guess. I've seen him around."

Jack remembered her from the previous summer when she'd brought a harassment charge against Martin Kilhooey, with whom she'd been living in the same apartment she was in now. Hardly necessary for the court to have issued an order of protection, since once Officer Barney Jackson of the Fort McBain Police Department had held Martin out the second story window by his ankles, Martin had pretty much resolved that he wouldn't be hitting Daisy again anytime soon.

-12-

Then there had been the little barroom disturbance later that same summer, which Jack had also prosecuted. Daisy had gotten a little loud and when the new part-time cop had asked for ID, she'd pulled out a hunting knife from her belt and said, "This is my ID!"

He also had a vague recollection of a perjury arrest on her rap sheet. THAT might come in handy later.

"So, Daisy, let's take this from the top, while I hunt and peck. Tell me the first time you saw Patty last night. Did you see her anytime before she fell down the stairs?"

"No. Other than at the store last night about nine. She was acting real weird."

"How so?"

"I don't know. Just weird. The things she was saying."

"Like what?"

"Just weird shit. Gave me the creeps."

"OK. Now did you see her leave the store? That's Larry's Market, right?"

"Yeah, Larry's. She bought one or two six-packs and I guess she went back upstairs to her apartment."

"How many apartments in that building?"

"Well, none on the first floor 'cause that's really the store. I'm on the second floor, and Eleanor Glaskey. Martin is right over me on the third floor and Patty's is over Eleanor's."

Bull leaned toward her and smiled. "Is Martin still your BOYFRIEND?"

"Martin Kilhooey can eat my shit."

"He'd probably like that."

Daisy laughed. "Yeah, he probably would."

"Now, when did you leave Larry's and where did you go next?"

"Well, Martin left first, then I went home a few minutes later. After a while Martin came down and asked if I wanted to play cards so we did for a while."

"Maybe he was just looking for something to eat." And Bull and Daisy laughed mirthfully together.

This is getting surreal, thought Jack Hughes, sitting in an office chair on Bull's right, facing Daisy with his legs crossed and his right wing-tip shoe pointing straight at her. He glanced at his foot . . . and there was this great gob of mayonnaise, blood and strawberry jam.

He quickly changed positions.

"So I take it at some point you left your apartment?"

"Yeah, about 11 or 11:30. Martin fell asleep on my couch so I went for a walk and went over to Marie Daley's house across the bridge. I stayed with her till about 1:15 then came home."

"OK, now who's Marie Daley and what the hell is she doing entertaining company at that hour?"

"Things don't start happening till after midnight. Don't you know that?"

"Guess that's why I keep missing everything," Bull sighed.

"Marie is my landlady's daughter, you know, Marge Brown."

"So whadya talk about for two hours?"

"Just bullshit. She finally kicked me out so I went home."

"And that's when you found the door blocked."

"Right."

"Now, you said Martin was there. He goed something and you goed something, remember?"

"Yeah."

"Now where did HE come from. Did he go over to Marie's too?"

"No, no. He was just out on the street, out for a walk, I guess. We musta got home about the same time."

"Now that's funny that he'd be out walking 'cause I heard he hurt his knee."

Daisy pondered. "Yeah, I guess that is pretty strange. He had a brace on his leg from a operation and couldn't get his right boot on so he was mostly walking around with a bread bag on his foot. But he's an asshole, so for him it's not really that strange, I guess."

"Yeah, he is an asshole, isn't he? You know what? I looked up asshole in the dictionary and right there next to the definition was a picture of Martin Kilhooey."

Daisy laughed. "I don't suppose you looked up 'pecker' in that dictionary."

"That's enough, Daisy. Let's get back to work before all those free palms are gone. Now, who went to call the ambulance?"

"I did. I went over to Carl Brown's house 'cause I saw the lights on."

"That's right next door?"

"Right. Actually I didn't go to call the ambulance, 'cause I didn't know about Patty yet. I was just looking for help to open the door."

"Couldn't Martin have helped you?"

"Maybe you should look up 'worthless piece of shit' in your dictionary too."

"So what was the worthless piece of shit doing while you were getting help?"

"I don't know. I don't think he was there when we got back, at least not right away."

"OK. Then what happened."

"After we found Patty, somebody, I think Andy or his girlfriend, ran back to call the ambulance and the girlfriend held Patty till the ambulance got there."

"Hey," said Bull, "I hear Andy's girlfriend's kinda cute."

"Yeah, I guess if you like that sort of thing," Daisy grinned.

"Well, I DO like that sort of thing," said Bull. "Think she'd like me?"

"Everybody likes you, Bull"

"Not everybody. Ever meet my supervisor Whelan Oates? His picture's right under Martin's next to the second alternative definition of asshole."

You just can't teach this kind of stuff, thought Jack.

Whelan Oates received the latest updates from the Sheriff.

"Want me to run out and interview Marie Daley?"

"No, Whelan, I'll take care of that myself. We've got some important things for you to attend to. Make sure the evidence gets logged in properly, very important. And you'll need to personally take care of Martin Kilhooey and make him comfortable till we can free somebody up to interview him. OK?"

Oates seethed. "Whatever you say. You are the Constitutionally Elected Sheriff of DeWitt County Emory Rushmore."

"And don't you forget it, young man."

No wonder they call him Auntie Em behind his back, grumbled Oates. *Not me, of course. Wouldn't be right. Play my cards right, that job'll be mine one of these days. Must be cool. Must be cool. Goddam Heimlich.*

"Martin, would you like a cup of coffee?"

"No thanks, Mr. Oates."

Well. Well. At least he called me Mister.

Chapter 2.

Marie Daley sat across her kitchen table from Sheriff Rushmore. She hadn't gotten much sleep, what with Daisy's visit and then her mother waking her up at God-knows-what hour demanding to know what Daisy had been doing at her house at one in the morning.

Like I'd be interested in Daisy. The thought made her shiver.

"We're just tying up some loose ends here, Mrs. Daley. We understand that Daisy Nichols might have been over here last night and we'd like to know whatever you can remember."

"Of course. Yeah, she was here. Scared the hell out of me, I'll tell ya."

She'd been babysitting Eleanor Glaskey's baby girl, keeping her overnight. She and husband Ed had just gone to bed when the doorbell rang, about 11:30. Ed threw some pants on and came back a few moments later. "It's Daisy. She wants to talk to you."

"Daisy, what is it? We were just going to bed!"

"Sorry to bother you, but I figured you might be up with the baby."

"Well, you figured wrong. What is it?"

Daisy shuffled her feet. "I think I owe your mother a door knob."

"A door knob? What the hell are you talking about?"

So Daisy tells her about the troubles she had with Patty, how the stupid bitch was making all kinds of weird noises and stomping around her apartment, and how it reminded her of a couple of weeks earlier when Patty had come home late from working the second shift and deliberately pounded her feet on the steps and hallway outside Daisy's apartment just to wake her up and annoy her.

Daisy had had enough. She ran up the stairs and beat her fists on Patty's door and demanded entrance. She heard Patty's voice asking why. "I want to talk to you, bitch!" Patty wouldn't open. Martin was right behind her.

"Martin, go get a screwdriver." So when Martin came back with the screwdriver, they did a major deconstruction on the door knob, not just carefully removing the screws but more like a pry-bar job, pushing and shoving and twisting and yanking until finally the whole cheap thing came apart. Now the door opened right up for them. Patty stood in her kitchen on the other side of the door.

Daisy wasted no time and clobbered her with a left hook to the side of her head. It drew blood, lots of it. "I'm sorry," Patty whimpered. "I only wanted you. I only wanted you."

"She was getting weird on me. I told her, 'I'm leaving and you'd better be gone when I get back'. Then the little wimp asks me *permission* to change her bloody clothes and put them in the sink. What an idiot!"

Daisy pulled a hunting knife off her belt, held it in her left hand and tapped it on the crook of her right elbow. "I was ready for her if she tried anything. I'm always ready."

Daisy was reluctant to leave Marie's house as it grew later and later. "The cops might be waiting for me."

"Don't worry about it," Marie advised. "You know Patty isn't gonna say anything. Go home. I'll stop by tomorrow to make sure you're ok."

"Yeah. And Martin knows what's good for him. He opens his trap and I'll take care of him good and he knows it."

So she left, sometime after one. It's a seven to ten minute walk from Daisy's to Marie's.

"Daisy, thank you very much. You've filled in a lot of details for us and I think now would be a good time for the Assistant District Attorney to get you a nice hot cup of coffee, right Jack, old buddy?"

Jack stood and walked toward the door. "Hey, one more thing as long as you're up. Grab me one too. And see if you can snarf a couple of donuts. And don't eat them all yourself, hear?"

Jack nodded, saluted, and exited.

"A couple of things we forgot to talk about. What happened when you got to the hospital, anything?"

"I was too upset about the whole thing so I stayed in the car. After a while Marge and Martin came back and said she was dead." Bull could detect not a trace of regret in her voice.

"That Patty, she was a strange one, wasn't she?" Bull suggested.

"A weirdo. I know you're not supposed to say anything bad about dead people, but . . ."

"Hey, this is an investigation. I think the rule gets suspended under these circumstances."

"Well, she's been kinda spaced out for the last couple of weeks, quit her job, sits in her room making all kinds of weird noises. Says weird shit. I wouldn't be surprised if she did this to herself."

"Really!" exclaimed Bull. "I don't know, though. Stabbing yourself in the leg is a pretty gruesome way to do yourself. She coulda stuck her head in the oven a whole lot easier."

"Well, she wasn't too bright. Besides, she was drunk all the time. Probably wouldn't have even felt it."

"That's true, that's true," Bull considered. "But if she did herself, where's the weapon? We didn't find anything and it hardly looks like she had time or energy to hide it."

"Maybe one of those kids took it. Or Martin."

"Yeah, maybe. Well, anything's possible. Right now the whole thing's a mystery. Martin own a knife?"

"I'm sure everyone has some kind of knife. I saw him cutting up cheese in his apartment earlier."

Bull laughed. "Wouldn't it be funny if that was it. I can see the tabloid headlines: 'The Cheese Knife Murder!'"

Daisy chuckled. "Yeah, well, as you say, anything's possible, especially with those characters."

"True, true," agreed Bull. "I'll bet even you own a knife or two."

"You know I do, Bull."

"Oh, yeah," said Bull, feigning remembrance, "'Dis is my ID!' That knife?"

"Yeah, that one."

"I notice you're not wearing it. I guess you know who you are today, right?"

"Right."

"So where's your knife?"

"Somewhere in my apartment, I guess. I usually just toss it when I come in. It's there someplace."

"That's cool. Just one other thing I think we forgot to talk about. That little squabble you had with Patty down in Larry's Market."

"That wasn't a squabble." Daisy stopped. "Who told you about that?"

"Oh, Marge mentioned it. Said you were ragging on her."

"Wasn't nothin'," Daisy said. "I was just asking her why she'd be so stupid as to quit her job. Stupid bitch."

"Well, it was pretty stupid, but why did that bother *you*?" Bull asked, sincerely.

"I got her the damn job and then when she does something stupid it make *me* look stupid and I don't like to look stupid."

"I hear ya." Just then the door opened and Jack entered balancing three cups of coffee and two donuts. He gave one cup and a donut to Daisy and placed a jelly donut and coffee in front of Bull. "I don't want a freakin' jelly donut.

Don't they have any of them French crullers or something. I love French, don't you Daisy?" She nodded at his very-nearly insubordinate leer. "Want something right, do it yourself. Don't trust some hotshot law-yer. Come on Jack, let me show you the fine art of selecting donuts. Excuse us, Daisy."

"Hey, Jack, don't you think a *jelly* donut might spook her?" Bull asked.

"Did you see my shoes?" The gob of mayonnaise and jam and blood was still there. Jack grabbed a napkin and mostly got rid of it, though it had hardened a bit and some remained in the little wing-tip holes.

They exchanged information over a slow cup of coffee and then another one.

There was a long silence. Finally Jack spoke. "Bull, if she had her knife at Marie's house, and she came back and the door was blocked and somebody was with her all the time and she doesn't have the knife now, how could it have gotten into her apartment, if it is there?"

"If it's there, old buddy, then I guess she must have put it there *before* she accidentally discovered the body, which means she was probably in the building when Patty was stabbed, which means she just might not be telling me the whole truth in there."

Sheriff Rushmore was making all reasonable efforts to maintain the fiction that this was an investigation by the Fort McBain Police Department, a department which consisted of a Chief, Harvey Wildman, three full-time officers and a handful of part-time "specials", and that the DeWitt County Sheriff's Office was merely assisting.

"Chief, do you have any officers available to talk to Martin Kilhooey?"

Chief Wildman smiled. "I've got just the guy. Barney Jackson just came on duty. I'll send him down to your office right away.

Officer Barney Jackson flung open the door.

"Hi, Martin. Remember me?" Martin Kilhooey pushed his body as far back into his chair as was possible.

"Now, Martin, I have been given the pleasant task of finding out from you exactly what happened last night. And before we start I have a few ground rules for you. Somebody read you your Mirandas?" Martin nodded. "Good, now, first off I don't want you to waste my time with bullshit. So, we are not going to begin this story with 'I came home from a walk and I found a body and I have no idea how it got there.' Understood?"

"Understood."

Martin, with a firm recollection of how far away the ground seems when dangling by your ankles out a second storey window, told his tale rapidly.

After coming upstairs from Larry's, Daisy agreed to play some cards with Martin. He hopped back up to his third-floor apartment, got the cards, and told Daisy how Patty was making all these strange noises.

"That's it! I've had enough of her shit!" So Daisy marched up the stairs and banged on the door. Patty wouldn't let her in. Then Daisy remembered she was storing a jar of mayonnaise and a jar of strawberry jam that belonged to Patty in her refrigerator because hers was on the fritz.

Again she pounded on the door, and again Patty wouldn't open it. "I've got your jam and your mayonnaise, you bitch! Open up!"

"Keep them. I don't want them anymore!"

And with that Daisy stood back from the door and hurled them, one in each hand, with all her might. They shattered near the top of the door and a gooey blend of red and off-white globbed down the door and settled on the floor with the broken glass and the rest of the mess.

Still the door remained closed, so she returned to her apartment yet another time and got a screwdriver while Martin stood in the doorway of his own apartment watching as she pounded and pried and pulled and swore and kicked till finally the whole thing burst apart and the door opened.

Patty just stood there helpless as Daisy hauled back and belted her on the side of the head. There was blood everywhere. "Daisy, don't hurt her!" pleaded Martin, but it was too late and Daisy turned toward him. "Keep your fucking trap shut or you're next!"

He thought things had calmed down after Patty begged permission to change her clothes. Daisy let her go back to her easy chair in the living room where she'd been watching tv. Then Daisy moved towards her. "How can one person be so fucking stupid? Stay away from Marge, do you hear me? She's not interested in you or your fucking mental problems!"

"I just wanted you, Daisy. All I ever wanted was you."

"That's it you fucking weirdo!" and as Daisy raised her fist again Patty suddenly reached for the snack table next to her and started hurling beer bottles at her attacker. One was nearly full and shattered all over the wall behind the television, just missing Daisy's head. Daisy whipped out her knife and slashed at Patty's chest. More blood. Martin grabbed her. "STOP!!"

Daisy screamed at Patty, "You are out of here tonight! You'd better be gone by the time I get back or you've had it!" and she stormed out the room, yelling to Martin as she left, "I don't know about you, but I'm getting the fuck out of here."

Martin stayed behind and helped Patty clean herself up. Then, still hobbling around, he cleaned up the hallway a little, brought Patty another six-pack and went back down to Daisy's apartment and fell asleep on her couch watching tv.

Then, a little after one she came back. In a fury. Flying up the stairs.

There were no screams, none at all, and suddenly Patty appeared, crawling down the third floor hall, covered in her own blood now rapidly leaving her. She pulled herself up, leaned on the rail and headed down. When she reached Daisy's door Martin tried to get in front of her but she brushed him aside and then tumbled down the first flight of stairs landing headfirst and unconscious at the front door.

Martin waited for nothing. Brace or no brace he jumped over the body, forced open the door and took off into the street. He hung around the neighborhood, lurking in the shadows, until Daisy came out. She found him.

"Here's the deal. We were both out and got home at the same time. We tried to open the door but something was blocking it. We don't know *anything*. Understand?"

Martin understood. When Daisy went next door for help, Martin skulked back into the alley, where he remained until the ambulance arrived.

"Good. Very good, Martin," said Officer Jackson. "Now let's go over it again."

"Sorry we took so long, Daisy. Once you get your hands on a donut box, it's a little hard to let go. Want another one?" Bull asked.

"No thanks. We almost done?"

"Pretty much. I'm wondering if you have any objection if we search your apartment?"

"Why?" Daisy asked more than a little warily.

"We're trying to locate every knife in the building so the coroner can rule them out or in. You said you had one, we know you have one, you told me you had nothing to do with this and we want to help you prove it. Will you go for it?"

Daisy squirmed. "Do I have a choice?"

Jack interjected. "Of course you have a choice. The Bill of Rights guarantees you to be free from unreasonable searches and seizures. You say no, and we have to prove to a judge that we have a good reason to conduct a search of your apartment."

"The key word here," said Bull, "is 'unreasonable'. Now, here we have blood over three floors, there's four apartments, nobody else inside, and a body at the foot of the stairs. Now, there's got to be a sharp instrument someplace. Do you think it's unreasonable that we would want to look everywhere in the building?"

-22-

"I guess not," Daisy muttered. "Go ahead and do it."

"Now," said Jack, "I have here a waiver form that gives the Sheriff and the Fort McBain Police permission to search your apartment. This paper gives them exactly the same authority as if they got a search warrant from a judge. If you have no objection, then you can read it over and sign it. If you *do* have an objection, then don't sign it, and if you have any questions about this, I'll try to answer them as best I can."

"No, that's ok. I'll sign. Give me the paper." She signed.

"Now I'd appreciate it very much if you'd stay here for a while longer," Bull requested amicably. "We're still waiting for some information from the field and there's a few more things you might be able to help us with. Besides," he smiled, "it's gonna be a few more hours before they let anybody back in the building anyway."

"Whatever you say." She was showing signs of weariness. She felt that slowly, but surely, she was losing this fight.

"One more thing. Do you have the keys to your apartment? It would make it easier."

"No, Bull. Stupid me, I left the keys on the table inside the door and locked it behind me without thinking."

I wonder when she did that, thought Jack. His head was spinning.

Officer Sherwood Gray, FMBPD, was pulling guard duty when Bull and Jack arrived at Daisy's apartment. When the three of them stood outside the second floor locked door, Jack suddenly caught a whiff of natural gas. It seemed to be coming from Daisy's door.

"Shut the lights off," Bull barked. "Turn off the portables," he yelled upstairs where the technicians were still working. "Sherwood, run next door and call Niagara Mohawk and see if they can shut off the gas to this place. Then see if the landlady's got an extra key."

He turned to Jack. "We can't knock the door in. A spark might set off the gas."

A few minutes later Andy Brown came up the stairs. "Grandma says she doesn't have a key handy. But there is another way to get in."

"How?" asked Bull.

"The hallway window leads to the roof over the store. You can follow that around and then climb in a window."

Jack immediately threw open the window and climbed out. Bull hesitated. "Stay there. I'll open the door from the inside," Jack shouted.

He located the window to the kitchen/living room quickly and found the aluminum storm came off easily. He pushed up the inside window, took a deep breath and rather awkwardly stumbled over the battered couch and onto the floor. He located the gas stove, shut off all the valves and opened the hall door.

It was blasted hot, probably about 90, and the oven had been on and open. Some pieces of uncooked chicken lay decaying on top of the stove. It looked like someone had left in a hurry.

Bull found the missing keys quickly and supervised two other deputies in a careful search. When all the exposed areas had been covered, yielding only a pair of scissors and a small pocket knife which was exactly where Daisy had told Bull it would be, they turned to the unexposed areas, drawers, cabinets and the clothes closet.

Bull lifted the mattress up. "Well looky here. What does that look like, Jack?"

"Sure looks like a hunting knife, or at least a sheath for a hunting knife with what appears to be a handle of said knife exposed to view," he said more particularly. And so it appeared, lying between the mattress and box spring. Bull called for a photograph.

When all the shots had been taken, distant, medium and closeup, Bull pulled out a handkerchief and carefully pulled on the handle and exposed what certainly appeared to be a blade. It was moist with what looked like steam on a mirror, which disappeared as they watched.

"Looks like blood near the hilt," noted Bull.

"I think I may have a few more questions for Daisy."

Sheriff Rushmore was just leaving the home of the ambulance driver who confirmed the story of Daisy attempting to climb in the back with Patty and jumping out of the vehicle, and also that he had been the one who demanded Daisy's name and address at the hospital. He had given the Sheriff the paper with "Polly Eckler" written on it.

Rushmore was traveling north on the Cooperstown Road toward Fort McBain. "1-0-1 to Dispatch" he barked into his microphone.

"Go ahead, Sheriff."

"Departing location, heading for Fort McBain P.D., ETA five minutes."

"Code 4."

The road was clear and dry, the morning beautiful with blue sky driving the last of the snow clouds over the eastern horizon. Emory Rushmore began to relax for the first time in the last nine hours. He knew these roads like the back of his hand, having spent thirty-six years in law enforcement in this county, a good portion of it patrolling the highways and back roads near Fort McBain. Coming up was a big wide curve, re-engineered a decade earlier by the State Highway Department to eliminate its far more dangerous predecessor.

He couldn't see around the bend, of course, so he had no way of knowing that even a "safe" highway can be dangerous if occupied by a vehicle in the wrong lane, like the old white van now heading south. When they were suddenly face to face he instinctively knew what to do.

His years of training and experience told him that to do nothing meant death for all concerned, so he pulled his unmarked car sharply to the right, off the shoulder, down a small embankment, and into a waiting tree.

The white van slowed, then moved on.

Chapter 3.

Jack Hughes enjoyed the moment.

"You know, old buddy, that was a pretty smooth move you made leaping out that window like some freakin' super-hero," remarked Bull on the short ride back to the police station. "You know, though, that's really the kind of stuff *cops* should be doing, not fancy hot-shot law-yers."

Jack turned toward his friend with smug satisfaction. "In the criminal justice system, the People are represented by two separate yet equally important groups: me and me."

"Gotta hand it to you, you're doing it all today."

"You're not doing so bad yourself. Now turn that old charm on Daisy and let's wrap this thing up."

"So, Daisy, we have the knife," Bull intoned solemnly, "and we're pretty sure we know how it got there. Are you ready to tell us the rest of the story?"

"I don't know what you mean," Daisy tried lamely.

"Well, first off we know that you told your friend Marie that you owed her mother a doorknob and that you powed Patty on the side of her head and that there was blood all over the place. Ya wanta start there?"

Daisy sat motionless trying desperately to think, think, think her way out of this.

"Or maybe you could tell me about the mayonnaise and the strawberry jam."

Daisy shifted. "That was an accident."

"Tell me."

"I went to bring her that stuff, 'cause it was hers, and she opened the door suddenly and knocked them out of my hands. It wasn't my fault."

"Daisy, I saw the door. That stuff was all over the door from the top to the bottom."

She thought quickly. "The way the door hit me, they must have gone flying upward. That's all I can figure. I'm telling the truth. If Jesus Christ was standing right here I'd tell him it was the truth."

Suddenly the door flung open. Whelan Oates. "Bull I need to see you

NOW."

An anonymous phone call had sent the Sheriff's road patrol out looking for an accident on the Cooperstown Road. At first, the Deputy missed it. There were no skid marks to lead him over the hill, but on his way back down the road he noticed the disturbed vegetation and found the car and the Sheriff. He was alive, barely, and in a few minutes every available law enforcement agency and emergency group had been summoned. Unconscious, he would soon be air-lifted to a regional hospital specializing in trauma cases.

"For now, Bull, I'm in charge. Did you get a confession yet?" inquired Acting Sheriff Oates.

"Not quite. I think she's ready to go for it, probably would have had it if you hadn't come storming in here."

"I've had enough of your insubordinate crap, Heimlich. If you haven't got a confession after all this time, you're not doing something right. You're off the case."

"WHAT!!"

"You heard me. Go back to the office and see if you can figure out what happened to Auntie Em!" Oates blanched with horror as the words escaped his lips. "I mean, the sheriff," he muttered. "Anyway, I'll take over here. Get going."

Bull stared for a moment, the rage building. Then he turned and left without a word, glancing at the baffled Jack Hughes on his way out the door.

"Miss Nichols, my name is Whelan Oates and at the moment I am the Acting Sheriff of DeWitt County. I don't know what Investigator Heimlich has been telling you, but we know you committed this murder and you might just as well confess so it'll go easier on you. Now, is there anything you'd like to say?"

Daisy raised her head and looked him square in the eye. "Yes, Mr. Oates, there is something I'd like to say. Two things, in fact. First, I know where to find your picture in the dictionary. And second, I want to talk to a lawyer."

Jack Hughes was totally disgusted. The magic words, "I want to talk to a lawyer" meant that nothing she said after that could be used against her, unless a lawyer was present. "That's it for me," he said and stomped out the door right into the arms of the District Attorney.

"Mr. Hughes, we need to talk," said the District Attorney.

"Why wasn't I notified of this murder before nine o'clock this morning?" demanded the District Attorney.

"They told me there was no answer at your house, so they called me. That's all I know."

"And nearly six hours go by and you don't think to send a car out looking for me?"

Jack shuffled. "Hey, things were a little hectic here. I didn't realize nobody was taking care of that."

The District Attorney was turning white hot, a barely controlled fury. "Meanwhile, you're here making serious decisions for my office. Do I understand that you personally authorized a search waiver on the Nichols apartment?"

"Yes, sir. Or at least, I reviewed it."

"On WHOSE AUTHORITY?" screamed the D.A. "*I* am the District Attorney of DeWitt County. *I* make all the decisions on felony cases. *You* were hired to handle traffic tickets and misdemeanors, not murder cases!"

"You weren't here! What was I supposed to do, NOTHING?"

"That's right. You do *nothing* unless I tell you to do it."

Jack gritted his teeth. "Is there anything you'd like me to do now?"

"Nothing," said the District Attorney.

Jack thought of Bull, then checked his watch. "Still time to get some of those free palms," he said and went home to his family.

"She asked for a lawyer," Acting Sheriff Oates told the District Attorney, "So we better get her one so I can continue with my interrogation."

"There is absolutely no way any competent attorney is going to let her talk to us," the District Attorney slowly explained so it might sink into Whelan Oates' thick skull.

"So," Oates grinned, "why don't we get her an *in*competent attorney?"

The District Attorney considered it, then considered again. "How well do you know the Town Justices here?"

"Fred Lawton is my wife's uncle."

"Talk to him."

Fred Lawton understood immediately. He was a retired state trooper, used to the ways of the real world, not that namby-pamby fictional world of the Warren Court, *dumb bastards I hope they all get mugged in hell.*

He looked over the list of attorneys available for assigned counsel and frowned. There were some pretty dumb ones there, but none that dumb. The only possibility was this new name on the list, a female lawyer from a neighboring county. According to his records she'd only been admitted to practice for two years and had never appeared in DeWitt County. And being a woman, she wouldn't know much about criminal law, he was sure of that.

"I think I'll be giving Miss Lynn Reynard a call."

The District Attorney introduced himself and was happy to do so. This Lynn Reynard was more than a little attractive. The medium length blond hair flowing freely, but neatly, the perfectly manicured nails, the crisp tailored suit, the full lips and mostly the entrancing green eyes made for an overall pretty positive first impression.

"It's a pleasure to meet you. I've heard a lot about you," she smiled.

"All good, I hope," he answered cleverly.

"Of course," she replied sweetly.

Whelan Oates walked in.

"And this is Whelan Oates from the Sheriff's Department. He's conducting the investigation."

"Acting Sheriff Whelan Oates, ma'am," fumbled Acting Sheriff Oates.

She stuck out her hand and grabbed his. "Nice to meet you, Whelan. And cut out the ma'am stuff. Call me Lynn." Her eyes sparkled. *Just for me*, he thought. *Wow*.

"Well, Lynn," said the District Attorney, "if I may call you Lynn also?"

"Of course."

Oates stomach sank just a little.

"Lynn, your client may have been involved as a witness or participant in a murder and we'd like to continue talking to her to clarify some things we've learned otherwise. Is it ok with you if we just get started?"

"Of course it's not ok," she laughed and tapped him lightly on the arm. "You are such a tease. Don't I get to at least talk to my client first in this county?"

Oates and the District Attorney looked at each other.

"Of course!" they both said simultaneously.

Forty-five minutes later Lynn Reynard finished her discussion with Daisy Nichols and politely told the waiting gentlemen that there would be no further talking to her client today.

"I guess you'll have to charge her or release her!" she noted breezily.

The District Attorney had been using the time to review the evidence.

"Charge her," he ordered Oates.

"Actually, it's not technically our case," he said. "This is a Fort McBain P.D. case."

And so it was that on Palm Sunday, 1999, after one hour and a half of mostly hunting and a little pecking, Chief Harvey Wildman produced a Felony Complaint charging Daisy Nichols with "mudder in the second degree."

At the arraignment before Justice Lawton Attorney Reynard entered a perfunctory "Not Guilty" plea and demanded a felony hearing within seventy-two hours, said goodbye to her client and promised to meet with her the next day at the jail.

"I hate blondes," said the District Attorney.

"Me, too," said Acting Sheriff Whelan Oates.

Bull Heimlich listened to the tape of the 911 call on the sheriff's accident. He didn't have to listen a second time.

"Max Lester," he said. "Drives an old beat-up white van that he uses in his junking business. Pick him up."

Within the hour Max had told him the whole story, how there was too much play in his steering wheel, how he tried to compensate and ended up overcompensating (not Max' word, being about three syllables too long for him) and went flying into the wrong lane going around the curve. He had no idea the unmarked car carried the sheriff, and felt especially bad about that because the sheriff had saved him from drowning once when he was a kid and his parents weren't paying any attention as he played on the rocks by the river in back of the Hunter Tavern.

Bull charged him with felony leaving the scene, had him arraigned before a Town Justice who sent him to jail without bail, and finally, finally went home and caught a three hour nap, muttering the name of Whelan Oates every so often. When he awoke he found his wife had laid one of those free palms across his chest.

Chapter 4.

Monday, March 29, 1999, 0700

T he ringing phone pierced Jack Hughes' skull. He fumbled over his pregnant sleeping wife and grabbed it.

"H'lo," he murmured.

"Jack, old buddy! How'd all that make you feel yesterday?" Bull Heimlich inquired brightly.

"Oh, pretty lousy. How about you?"

"Same here! Ya know, there's only one cure for this."

"An electric enema for our bosses?" suggested Jack.

"Nope. Thunder Run."

"I'm in."

So within the hour Jack had thrown his scuba gear in the back of his eight-year-old SUV, kissed his thirty-two-year-old wife and three-year-old daughter goodbye, grabbed a bottle of five-year-old brandy, picked up his thirty-four year-old friend, and headed for Gold Harbor, Maine and the hundred and nine-year-old Gold Harbor Beach Inn.

They secured a room on the beach (not much action in March), filled two gallon jugs with hot water, donned their wet suits and gear, poured the hot water into the suits to help balance the action of the cold ocean water, and plunged straight in off the beach, inflated their buoyancy compensators, floated on their backs until they reached the foot of the high cliffs overlooking the entrance to the protected cove, purged the air from the BC's and sank slowly to the bottom.

It was a cold but sunny day and the surf gentle. They were in water thirty feet deep, exploring the rocks around the base of the cliff. Visibility excellent.

Full wet suit or no, the first impact of March North Atlantic brine hitting your face can be bracing, and the neoprene boots never seem quite enough. Still, Jack loved it. There was a certain peace beneath the waves. Some folks get panicky under water, but for Jack the soft undercurrents, the buoyancy, the free-floating bubbly world and the near-silence resembled the security of the womb.

Not much wildlife, just an occasional fish, a few hermit crabs, some small lobsters strictly off-limits. Jack liked reaching out to those stringy-wavy things that hang on rocks and close right up when you touch them. He didn't know what they were called, nor even if they were animal or vegetable, he just liked to watch the way they instinctively retreat into themselves when sensing danger. Sort of like Daisy Nichols, he thought, but let it pass quickly.

They always carried "goody bags" on these dives, because you never knew what "treasures" you might find on this ancient coast which once was rumored to harbor pirates and smugglers. Mostly the treasures were fishing lures, old bottles, sand dollars, and various twentieth century garbage. There were occasionally coins, thrown off the cliff for good luck on special occasions from the highest spot overlooking the Atlantic at the end of a long footpath that meandered above the south end of the cove.

With the bright sunlight and relatively clear water, it was a good day for treasure hunting and they each managed to find a few corroded coins of limited value.

Then Jack spotted a glint, pulled out his sea knife to investigate, and excavated from the sea bottom a pair of dog tags, like the kind his father had brought home from World War II. He scraped them off a bit with the knife, then carefully added them to his treasure, along with a couple of pretty little shells for his pretty little daughter and his pretty little wife.

By and by they made their way back to the beach and the Inn, rinsed off their gear, took hot showers and moseyed into town for a bite to eat, dropping off their tanks at the dive shop for refilling. Over lunch they examined the day's loot.

"See, I like stuff like that," said Bull, eyeing the dog tags. "Isn't worth anything, probably, but its got a story attached to it. We don't know what it is, so that makes it a mystery story, and I like mysteries."

"Well," said Jack, "we know this guy had a name and a date of birth. Maybe he's alive, maybe he's dead. He was in the service."

"Maybe he liked it, maybe he hated it," added Bull. "If he's like most guys, it was a lot of both. How did the tags get in the water? Did he throw them in disgust to wipe out a bad memory?"

"Or," said Jack the misty-eyed romantic, "did someone important in his life hike out to the top of the cliff and toss them out to sea as a final remembrance of their undying love?" He sighed.

Bull lowered his voice. "Do you want me to kiss you now?"

Jack tossed a bag of french fries in his face, "You know, you can really be a jerk sometimes," and they both laughed.

"So, what do we do with this stuff, these worthless mysterious treasures of ours?" asked Jack. "I know my wife won't let me come home with any junk. She has very strict rules about such things."

"WHIP whip whip whip WHIP," said Bull.

There were no more french fries.

"Seriously, old buddy, I got just the thing. And we don't even have to leave the lobby of the hotel, " intoned Bull. "Sally O'Brien, who runs the place, has a collection of oddball stuff brought up by divers off the beach and keeps it in a big display case across from the fireplace."

"Perfect."

"Sally, old sweetheart, we've got some treasures to add to your *potpourri*," Bull schmoozed, handing over the loot.

"Another twelve cents in useless change I probably don't need, but I'll take it. Now these dog tags, first time for something like that, I think." She promptly marched over to the large display case and with a little gentle shoving of other stuff managed to display them reasonably prominently.

Bull and Jack looked over the junque-de-la-mer. Most of it made their stash look pretty good. Except for one item.

"Look at this," said Jack. "A class ring. Another mystery."

"I think I threw my class ring in the water someplace, too," said Bull, "or else I left it with an old girlfriend. I forget which." He picked the ring out of the case and gave it the once over.

"I think mine's wrapped in a dust ball behind my computer desk. Stopped fitting about my second year of college. I guess they shrink," said Jack, now looking closely at the ring himself.

"Bishop McClure High School, 1969," he read. "Looks like a girl's ring. Initials inside look like 'FS' but I can't be positive."

"Hey, Sally," yelled Bull across the lobby to the manager who was busy doing manager stuff again, "you know anything about a Bishop McClure High School?"

Sally looked up. "Sure. It was a regional Catholic high school about four miles up the road from here. Closed about ten years ago. One of my nieces went there. I think they're using it for some kind of day program for the retarded now."

Jack tossed the ring back. "Well, another mystery for another day."

After sunset they dove again, this time toward the center of the cove, to observe the strange world of bioluminescence and the fascinating beauty of jellyfish curiously glowing in their flashlight beams.

Later they laid a fire in the fireplace in the lobby, which they had to themselves, opened the brandy and sang Irish songs of rebellion and lost love. Jack was only 3/8 Irish, and from both sides of the great cause, and Bull not at all, but with the brandy and the fire and the events of the weekend and the sounds and the smell of the vast ocean and the melancholy of absence, however brief, from their loved ones, they felt very Irish tonight. Very Irish indeed.

When the last betrayal had been avenged and the last tear shed for the bonnie Irish lasses, they hit the sack, arising at 5 a.m. for the return Thunder Run, leaving foam and tide and the mysteries of the deep and the dog tags and the ring behind them.

By 10:30 Tuesday morning they were back to work.

Chapter 5.

Sheriff Rushmore was still in the special care unit, but had regained consciousness and his prognosis was improving with each passing hour. Still, the drugs alone prevented him from assuming any of his duties and Whelan Oates remained the Man of the Hour, briefing the press on both the murder investigation and the Sheriff's accident and condition. Bull Heimlich's name, of course, was never mentioned. Ever. Both matters, as far as the public knew, were joint ventures of Acting Sheriff Whelan Oates and the District Attorney. Whelan had been careful, however, to mention the small but significant role the Sheriff had played before the accident.

At the request of the District Attorney, the felony hearing in the case of *The People of the State of New York versus Daisy Nichols* took place on Tuesday evening, nearly a full day before necessary. The District Attorney did not want to give the blond Ms. Reynard any extra time to prepare. Also, at his request, Bull Heimlich prepared the witnesses, with the assistance of Assistant District Attorney Jack Hughes, in the Town Assessors office, located a short distance down the hall from the meeting room/courtroom in the Town of Landon Highway Department building on the Cooperstown Road.

The Defense strategy in a felony hearing is to find out as much about The People's case as possible. It is almost never to establish that there is insufficient evidence to hold the defendant for action by the Grand Jury, though that is the stated purpose of the hearing.

The People, on the other hand, try to hold back as many cards as possible, so as not to commit too much too soon, particularly when the case is still under investigation. Here, the autopsy had been performed on Monday while the prep men had been enjoying the Maine deep, but many of the lab test results had not been delivered, fingerprint analysis might take weeks, and even the contents of the victim's apartment had not yet been thoroughly inventoried, since Whelan, in the urgency of assuming his new duties had neglected to either complete or reassign some of his own.

Therefore, the District Attorney intended to limit his proof to the certified death certificate, the testimony of Marge Brown concerning the argument in the store, the testimony of Marie Daley concerning the admissions made at her home by the defendant, and the testimony of Martin Kilhooey placing the defendant in or near Patty Hartwick's apartment at the time she stumbled down the stairs.

After interviewing Martin Kilhooey, Heimlich and Hughes knew they had a problem and sent a note to the District Attorney asking for a short recess.

"Boss," said Jack, "you can't put Martin on the stand. His story is different every time he tells it. So far we don't have a written statement from him, but we know what he told Barney Jackson. The latest is he was taking a crap in his own apartment and didn't hear anything, came out and Patty brushed past him on the third floor, not the second, and isn't sure where Daisy was at that point, only that she came down after him, but it could have been from her own apartment rather than Patty's."

"Terrific," said the D.A. "Forget him then. We'll explain the facts of life to him before the Grand Jury meets."

When The People rested after calling only two witnesses and producing the death certificate, Attorney Reynard jumped to her feet.

"Your honor, I move to dismiss the charge and that the defendant be released immediately. She has been charged before this court with murder in the second degree," she continued, kindly overlooking Chief Wildman's spelling, though a couple of deputies in the courtroom gave each other knowing looks, "and all The People managed to show is that Patricia Hartwick is dead and that she might have exchanged words with the defendant earlier in the evening and that the defendant might have hit her. There is absolutely nothing connecting the defendant to any homicide.

"With respect to the alleged hitting, all The People have to support that is the uncorroborated oral statement allegedly made by the defendant and as a matter of law a person can not be convicted solely on uncorroborated statements against penal interest. Therefore, The People, from a legal standpoint, have proved nothing at all here tonight. Nothing. The defendant must be released. Thank you." She stood erect and confident for an instant and sat down.

The District Attorney responded. "Your honor, as counsel very well knows, a felony hearing is not the same as a trial. We do not need to prove each and every element of every charge beyond a reasonable doubt. Nor do we have to prove to any degree the specific charge which is the subject of the felony complaint. It is enough that we are able to show that *a* felony has been committed and that it is likely that the defendant committed the felony.

"We do not even have to enumerate what that felony was, but I can suggest to the court that we have shown that the defendant likely committed the felonies of Assault in the Second Degree, Assault in the First Degree, Criminal

Trespass, several degrees of Burglary, the defendant having unlawfully entered premises, being a dwelling, and at night, with the intention of committing a crime therein, and we also believe we have connected the defendant to the crime charged, murder in the second degree. Thank you."

"The Court finds that The People have shown that a felony has been committed and that it is likely that the defendant committed the felony. Accordingly, the defendant is held for action by the grand jury of this county and is remanded to the custody of the Sheriff of this county pending such action, without bail. The Clerk of the Court is directed to furnish a copy of this order and a record of all proceedings to the Clerk of the County of DeWitt," read Judge Lawton from a preprinted card he used to conclude all felony hearings.

Lynn Reynard whispered briefly to her client, who was then taken away by two sheriff's deputies and a matron.

A few minutes later the lawyers and remaining law enforcement personnel exchanged pleasantries in the parking lot.

"Nice job by The People," sparkled Attorney Reynard.

"Thank you, Lynn," replied the District Attorney. "I don't think you've met my assistant, Jack Hughes, and this is Investigator Walter Heimlich from the Sheriff's office."

"WALTER?" exclaimed Lynn. "I thought you were all Bull, and something else, too, according to my client," she twinkled.

"Just call me Bull, ma'am."

"OK, Bull. But cut out the ma'am. It's Lynn."

"Yes, ma'am," Bull replied. She ignored it.

"And you, Mr. Hughes, from what I've been hearing about you I pictured someone a trifle more athletic-looking, but obviously you can perform when the occasion arises."

"Yes, ma'am. When the occasion arises I'm up for the task," said Jack.

And suddenly in his head arose a roaring CLANG CLANG CLANG CLANG CLANG, those special alarm bells that conscience employs as a final warning to those about to step over the brink.

"I see you're not wearing your wing-tips tonight."

And now she was just plain glowing at him, locked eyes and all, and what eyes, and that smile and . . . and he began to wonder if she might want a beer for the road and was about to suggest it even, oblivious, completely oblivious that he had a home and a wife and a child and another on the way and that everyone else was still there, staring at him, until Bull tugged his sleeve.

"Come back to the office with me, Jack, we got a few things to go over."

"Alright, Walter."

She was still looking at him.

"Goodnight, Miss Reynard."

"Lynn."

Bull laughed hysterically. "Jack, old buddy, I have *never* seen you act like that. 'I'm up for the task'," and he fell on his office floor and clutched his gut and rolled and laughed till the tears ran and still he couldn't stop.

Jack was offended. "You know, before I met my wife, I'd been around a little." That only started Bull up again and now he was rolling from one end of the office to the other.

So Jack let him roll and when finally he had nothing left, a long time later, Jack said, "Seriously, Bull, that woman is dangerous. I think we need to find out about her. At this point we know absolutely nothing. Knowing your opponent is extremely important when trying a case."

"Jack, if it's her phone number you want, I'm sure she'll give it to you if you ask. If the occasion arises."

And there was no point in discussing it any further because Jack knew that if this insane laughter continued poor Bull would be having tea parties on the ceiling, and even though it would serve him right, he was still his friend.

"Goodnight, Walter."

When Jack got home he found his wife on the couch watching television. He made two cups of tea, snuggled in next to her and for the next hour they felt each other's closeness, her head resting comfortably on his shoulder as it always had and always would, until at last she took him by the hand and led him to their wonderfully familiar bedroom, where they enjoyed each other without even the slightest worry about getting pregnant.

Before going home Acting Sheriff Whelan Oates, feeling exceptionally generous, bought Miss Reynard a beer. He did his best not to tell her too much about the case, but his best was not too good. He only had one beer, but when he helped her with her coat and got close enough to smell her hair, he found himself more than a little intoxicated with Miss Lynn Reynard.

"You know, Whelan, there's something about you. I don't quite know what it is yet, but there's something you do that makes me feel like a teenager. Thanks for a lovely evening." And she kissed him on the cheek.

I've still got it, he thought.

Bull Heimlich almost didn't go home, then changed his mind. As he climbed into bed with his sleeping wife, he tapped her on the shoulder.

"You know," he said, "You ain't so bad."

"Most times you're not so bad yourself, Bull."

And feeling a certain satisfaction with that, he rolled over and went to sleep. She shook her head and did the same.

Chapter 6.

On the forty-fourth day after her arrest, the Grand Jury of DeWitt County returned a five-count indictment in the case of *The People of the State of New York versus Daisy Nichols*, charging her with Murder in the Second Degree and two counts each of Assault in the First Degree and Burglary in the First Degree. Arraignment was scheduled for Friday, May 21, 1999 at 10 a.m. in the County Court of DeWitt County, Hon. Samuel R. Blaine presiding.

Judge Blaine, at 48, was already in his ninth year on the bench. A former boy wonder, he had scored a stunning upset running for District Attorney at 34 and had compiled a solid record of convictions including some high-profile cases. When his predecessor had been elevated to a vacant Supreme Court position, Sam Blaine was the obvious choice for a gubernatorial appointment and he ran unopposed for the ten year term.

Along the way he had managed to overcome the "carpetbagger syndrome" which is the proposition that you have to have been born and raised in DeWitt County to get any consideration from the voters. He had never stepped foot in this county until hired as an associate attorney in a Sanford Mills office right out of law school at 25. He learned enough in two years there to know that he didn't like working for anyone else, so he hung out his own shingle, joined the right organizations, made a small name for himself and then a bigger one and eventually completely captured the public imagination, such as it was in the small upstate New York county.

He had never married. There were a few possibilities earlier on, but they hadn't panned out. Maybe most women were simply reluctant in this liberated age to be hidden in his ever-larger shadow. Their loss, he thought, on those rare occasions when he thought about it at all.

Somewhere along the line he had started writing sonnets of his lost loves for his own amusement. After each relationship had skidded to its permanent end, he would enshrine the loser in his "Rogues Gallery", immortalized in 14 lines of rhymed iambic pentameter, with the exception of his favorite, which after only one quatrain concluded with a rhyming couplet:

> *You prob'ly think you rate a poem or two,*
> *But half of one is all I'll waste on you.*

Very satisfying. Very satisfying indeed.

But there had been many years now since the last entry, and he had grown accustomed to alone.

"This is the case of *The People of the State of New York versus Daisy Nichols*, indictment number 83-99," recited Judge Blaine for the record. "Let the record indicate the People are represented by the District Attorney and the defendant is present in the courtroom.

" Miss Nichols, it is my duty to inform you that the Grand Jury of this County has handed up an indictment against you charging you with a number of crimes, the most serious of which is Murder in the Second Degree. Did you receive a copy of that indictment?"

"Yes, your honor," Daisy replied as her attorney had instructed.

"In connection with this indictment you have the right to an attorney at every stage of this proceeding. I see you have someone here with you. Is this your attorney?"

Daisy nodded.

"Counsel identify herself for the record, please."

"Lynn Reynard, Bath Springs, New York, appearing for the defendant."

"Retained or assigned?" inquired the judge.

"Assigned by Justice Lawton of the Town of Landon."

"The assignment will continue. Does your client waive a reading of the indictment?"

"We waive a reading, your honor."

"Then as to the five counts of the indictment, how does the defendant plead?"

Attorney Reynard motioned to her client.

"Not Guilty," said Daisy Nichols in a firm voice.

"Not Guilty plea is entered. Anything for the People?" asked the Judge.

"Only that the People are ready for trial and that at this time I am serving notice on the defendant that the people intend to offer certain statements made by the defendant at trial and will offer evidence of certain eye-witness identification, and make demand for any notice of alibi by the defendant," said the District Attorney.

"Anything for the defendant?"

"Your honor," said Attorney Reynard, "we request 45 days for the purpose of making motions and discovery."

"Granted. Is there an application for bail?"

"Not at this time, your honor."

"Defendant is remanded to the custody of the sheriff pending trial or other disposition or application for bail." Down came the gavel, and up rose his eyes, and for the first time Judge Samuel R. Blaine got a real look at Lynn Reynard, Esq. And he very much liked what he saw.

When her client had left the courtroom, she asked permission to approach the bench. Not remarkably, it was granted.

She offered her hand in the usual fashion, which he took. "I just wanted to introduce myself. Thank you for continuing the assignment. I look forward to working with you. I've heard a lot about you."

"I don't doubt that you have," he assumed. "Anything we can do to assist you in learning the ways of this court we will do. My door is always open."

"Be careful what you offer," she laughed merrily. "I just might take you up on that!"

"Believe me, it will be a pleasure," offered Judge Blaine.

And there were no alarm bells going off, for Judge Samuel R. Blaine had advised his conscience of its requirement to remain silent long, long ago.

A week later, Attorney Reynard received a letter in the mail.

Dear Miss Reynard,
    I read in the paper that you are representing Daisy Nichols in her murder trial. You don't know me. I was Daisy's teacher twenty years ago when she was in first grade and there are a few things I think you ought to know. . .

"Now, Daisy, sit back in your chair like a good little girl."
"I can't."
Miss Hurley sighed. "It's only Wednesday. Please try not to be defiant until at least Friday this week."
"De- - fiant?"
"Just do as you're told. Sit back in your chair and take out your workbook."
"I can't, Miss Hurley."
"And why not, pray tell?"
The pale little girl looked down at her desk and said quietly, "Because it hurts."

The kind, matronly school nurse helped Daisy remove her blouse and suppressed a gasp. Her frail body was covered with welts and bruises. Her back carried the distinct imprint of a 2x4. What wasn't purple was flaming red and her arms, always covered by long sleeves in the warmest weather, bore several circular areas of scar tissue, the unique memento of deliberate cigarette burns.

We asked her what happened, of course, and at first she just sat there quietly and said she didn't want to get in trouble, but we both had a pretty good relationship with her and eventually she opened up.

Little Daisy tripped happily home from school wearing her brand-new Spring coat. She stopped along the way to chat with friends, petted a dog, and got talked into a kick-ball game on the lot behind the firehouse. It didn't matter much what time she got home because her mother didn't care. What did matter is that she managed to lose a button off the coat, and that mattered a lot. Mommy finally stopped the screaming and dragged Daisy by the wrist and tied her, coatless, to the pig sty and left her there as the sun set and she got colder and colder and colder. She dared not whimper, because she knew what happens to bad girls who cry, like the time she got spanked for breaking the drinking glass and she made the mistake of crying.

"I'll give you something to cry about!" and she tried to run but she was too little and she tried to wiggle away but she was too weak and Mommy picked her up and exposed her raw bottom and sat her on the hot stove. She could smell her own flesh burning, could smell it still as she shivered in the dark and it got colder and darker but she wouldn't cry.

Eventually Mommy brought her inside and sent her to bed without supper, couldn't stand the sight of her, wicked stupid brat who doesn't know enough to keep her buttons on her new spring coat, goddam stupid little bitch.

The next day she went back to the lot behind the firehouse and with the help of her friends found the button. She ran home smiling and triumphant.

"Look, Mommy, my friends found my button for me!"

"Who the fuck told you to tell every asshole in the neighborhood our business?! Who? You stupid little shithead, I'll tan your hide!"

And all the while she beat her, the cigarette dangling from the corner of her mouth, the stale booze lingering on every quick breath, all she could think of was how this worthless piece of shit had almost ruined her marriage.

Her husband was an idiot, but he could count, and he knew he had been nowhere around when his fourth child was conceived. He'd been out whoring for a couple of months, she thought bitterly, and you'd think he'd be a little more understanding, but he wasn't and the mere sight of this child enraged him, so it was a lot easier to just keep Daisy away from him. Things had never been the same between them after that, despite four more brats over the next four years.

And it's all her fault, this ungrateful little bitch. I'm gonna beat the crap out of her this time.

Daisy went hungry again and oh-so-quietly cried herself to sleep.

When the social workers came to investigate the mother said, "Take her! I can't do anything with her, stupid little brat." No abuse charges were filed, no lawyer appointed for the little girl; they just snatched her away from the only home she knew, and her siblings, and her neighborhood, and her school and placed her with strangers. Good people though they were, their job was to house her and clothe her and feed her, not to love her, and she spent the next eleven years of her life adequately housed and clothed and fed.

She rarely went home, and as the years passed the visits from her family were fewer and fewer until eventually they just stopped, though she continued to get age-inappropriate Christmas presents until she was kicked out of the system on her eighteenth birthday. Every two years the Family Court extended her placement, every two years her mother would tell the worker the time wasn't right yet for Daisy to come home. No one ever filed any petitions to terminate parental rights and free her for adoption, so she spent nearly her entire childhood living in her own solitary world. For years she was under the impression that she couldn't go home because she was bad. No one ever told her any different.

Miss Reynard, I don't know whether Daisy did this thing or she didn't, but if she did, there's more than a little blame to go around. For me, all I'll ever see is that frightened little girl with the bruises and the marks and the burns and those sad, sad eyes that were too afraid to cry.
Sincerely,
(Miss) Beatrice Hurley

There were some things that even Miss Hurley didn't know, thought Daisy as she read the letter her lawyer had shared with her.

Like how when she was desperate for any kind of affection her twelve year old brother would hold her and cuddle her and take her up to his room and play with her under the blankets and how he'd tickle her and make her laugh and feel all warm all over and how he'd touch her where he wasn't supposed to, but it made her feel wanted and close to him and they'd giggle and he'd make her touch him where she shouldn't and it became a big secret game and he did all those things and more and sometimes it hurt but he'd shush her and they kept doing those bad things for almost a year until Daddy found out and made him

-47-

stop.

And after that Daddy, who had always seemed to hate her, suddenly got very nice and he played those games with her too, almost right up to the day she got taken away. She never told anyone, ever, about this in all these years.

It was their secret.

Chapter 7.

Guilderland, NY
July 17, 1999

A belated high school graduation party for Jack's favorite niece, Anna, brought together members of the far-flung Hughes family at the home of Neil Francis Hughes, Jack's much older brother, in suburban Albany.

Jack was the youngest, by far, of the five siblings, having come in at the tail end of the baby boom in 1966. Neil, 48, had a very successful law practice as a partner in a big downtown Albany firm and four children of his own with his wife of twenty-one years.

"Uncle Jack!" squealed the effervescent Anna with delight, and gave him a big hug after which he gave her a big present, then stepped aside to let her hug Aunt Maria and little cousin Laura.

"When's the baby due, Aunt Maria?"

"Middle of September, and cut out this aunt stuff. I've got two sisters younger than you," said Jack's wife.

"Cool. Hey, we're all adults now, anyway." She twinkled. "I think I'll go see what Neil and Mary are up to. Oh, Neil!" She shouted to her father, "Look who's here! Jack and Maria!"

Neil gave his brother and sister-in-law and niece and child to be a big group hug.

"Glad you could make it, Little Bro. Help yourself to a brewski. Maria, I take it a soft drink for you?"

Maria sighed. "The one drawback of pregnancy, leaving behind my decadent two-beer-a-month lifestyle."

Jack had settled back with his third Harp when along came the teenage nephews, Eddie and Neil, Jr.

"Uncle Jack, I hear you're working on a murder case!" exclaimed Neil, Jr.

"Well, not so much any more, but at the beginning I was right there for it all."

And once again in his mind's eye, Jack was dashing out on the roof, looking exceptionally buff, and flying through the window to save his friends and doubtless hundreds of innocent civilians from the massive explosion that could have been caused by that leaky gas stove!

"Did you see a lot of blood and guts, Uncle Jack?" inquired Eddie the irrepressible.

"Ah, yes, lad. Well, not so much guts as blood. Blood everywhere. Blood . . .and mayonnaise!"

"That's gross!" said Eddie excitedly.

"When's the trial? You gonna be a witness?" asked Neil Jr.

"Probably October. And, yes, I expect I may be called as a witness."

Big Neil, taking a break from the hamburger flipping, sat down next to his brother.

"You know what Tuesday is, Jack?"

Jack thought about it. Hmm. July 20. "Not my anniversary, I hope?"

Neil replied, "Not your anniversary, but a very great anniversary. It'll be thirty years since men from the planet earth first walked on the surface of the moon."

"You remember that, Dad?" said Anna, now momentarily halting her flitting and sitting down with the rest.

"Yes, Anna. I remember."

And suddenly it was July 20, 1969 and young Neil Hughes, recent high school graduate, is about to miss it all. His job as the sole Sunday afternoon and evening announcer at Sanford Mills' only radio station means that he will not be present to witness the greatest live television event in history.

At the last minute, though, his step-grandfather's brother comes up with a long-abandoned black and white portable, and Neil sets it up in the newsroom. He remembers that he had seen a long flat antenna wire in the attic of the station, left over from those days in the late forties when the manager used to set up a microphone next to a television speaker and pirate broadcast the Friday night fights. The roof-top antenna still works.

Not much life in this cathode-ray tube. Barely any light on the screen with sunshine coming through the windows. But that will improve when darkness falls.

He checks the log and sees that nothing about the moon landing is scheduled. No, they were going to broadcast the Yankees/Washington Senators game.

Neil calls the station program director.

"You know, I really think we ought to carry the moon landing."

"The advertisers have already paid for the Yankee game, and we have a package deal with the Yankee network. We just can't mess that up," says the program director. "I'll tell you what, you monitor the news network, and when it gets down to where they'll be landing soon, switch over for a couple of minutes, then make sure you go right back to the game."

All afternoon the old AP teletype machine in the back room keeps setting off its loud news-flash bell, and Neil is glued to the ABC radio monitor, interrupting only long enough to throw on an occasional Genesee Beer commercial for the local breaks.

"Eagle, you are go for power descent."
"Fourteen thousand feet and coming down beautifully."
"Five hundred and forty feet." And now Neil says to hell with the Yankee game and throws the switch.
"Four hundred feet . . . face forward and hatch down . . ." crackles the steady voice across the ether.
"Two hundred and fifty feet . . .two hundred and twenty feet . . .coming down nicely.
"One hundred feet . . ." and now the whole world stops breathing.
"Seventy-five feet. . .
"Lights on. Forward. Forward. Good. Forty feet . . .picking up some dust . . .Faint shadow . . Drifting to the right a little.
"Contact light. Okay, engine stop. . .Engine arm off.
"Houston . . .Tranquillity Base here. The Eagle has landed."

And Neil Hughes, 18-year-old high school graduate tough guy, sitting all alone in a tiny radio station in upstate New York, sits and blubbers like a baby.

And when, a few minutes later he fulfills his obligation to the beer distributor and returns to the Yankee game, it turns out they hadn't missed much, because, of course, as the moment came, like everywhere else in the world, things just stopped and all eyes were glued on the electric scoreboard in Yankee Stadium and when he throws the switch back all Neil can hear is thunderous cheers that just won't stop and suddenly at the stadium a recording of *America the Beautiful* starts playing and people are crying and laughing and dancing and screaming their hearts out and Neil Hughes knows that if he lives to be a thousand he will never experience another moment like this and he savors it. He savors it.

And finally Phil Rizzuto says, "Holy cow! I don't know about you, but I'm all choked up!"

Several hours later, and now it's dark and the old picture tube lights up a little and Neil's namesake on the moon opens a little hatch and a camera springs to life and there he is at 10:56 P.M. EDT, one man, alone, stepping on the surface of the moon.

Just in time, too, for young Neil Hughes has to finish the broadcast day with the 11 o'clock news and the National Anthem.

He goes out into the parking lot and looks up at the clear night sky, all the stars in the heavens and that moon that could never, ever look the same again and then, off to the side, sees a small, red steady light.

Mars.

When he arrives home his parents are glued to the television and 3-year-old Jack is bundled up in a blanket, asleep on the floor in front of the tv. Neil wakes him.

"Jack, Jack. Look at the television."

Little Jack rubs his eyes and looks.

"I know you're awfully little, Jack, but look at this. Two men. . . two men are walking on the moon! Look at this Jack, and try to remember this, remember this for the rest of your life. Try to remember this, Jack. . . because you'll never see anything quite this wonderful ever again."

And a few moments later little Jack curls up comfortably in his brother's lap and returns to blissful sleep.

And never remembered.

"Hey, Big Bro, I'm sorry, but it was way past my bedtime," grinned Jack. "Besides, I've seen it on tv a gazillion times since."

"Not the same. Not the same." A bitter poignancy was beginning to overcome Neil.

"So, Dad, how come they don't go there any more?"asked Neil, Jr.

"Cheap visionless bastards!" explained Dad.

"Mr. Hughes, watch your language in front of the children," warned his wife.

"I'm sorry, dear, you're right. Children, I apologize for my language. Please forgive me. I meant to say 'Cheap visionless persons of uncertain ancestry.'"

"That's better." They all nodded their approval.

"Fact of the matter is, kids, that as far as I'm concerned, except for the birth, death and resurrection of Our Lord and Savior, that was the greatest thing that ever happened in the history of the world, and those morons in Washington threw it all away. Worthless offspring of disputed pedigree!" he elaborated.

"But what about taking care of the poor here on earth and education and stuff like that? Shouldn't we do that first?" Anna offered, modernly.

And it was the wrong thing to say, because now the rage began to come over him and maybe it was the beer talking, but probably not.

"The poor we will always have with us!" he roared. "But this, this was a time when all mankind joined together on a glorious adventure, led by the free and God-fearing American people. It wasn't a matter of military conquest or subjecting a people or seeking out selfish gain. It was about challenge and discovery and excitement and small men with giant ideas facing the vast emptiness of the universe. It was about learning and seeing and being and believing in something bigger than yourself. It was about the human race after hundreds of thousands of years of evolution rising up out of this primordial swamp, reaching out and touching the face of God!"

And there was a great silence.

Until Neil, Jr said, "Get ya another Harp, Pops?"

"Of course."

Still later, when Jack found himself alone with his brother again, they began to reminisce about the family and their late parents and other relatives now gone. Neil remembered them a lot better, of course. Jack had been only eight when their father died and only vaguely remembered their father's mother.

"Gramma was Brooklyn Irish, the loveliest lilt in her voice. I doubt that she ever had an untroubled moment in her life, but she never showed it. She was always laughing and joking and singing. She used to sing you to sleep with those old Irish songs."

Hmmm. That might account for the way I get sometimes, thought Jack.

And now Neil threw his head back and started singing.

> Red is the rose that in yonder garden grows,
> Fair is the lily of the valley,
> Clear is the water that flows from the Boyne,
> But my love is fairer than any.

"Wait a minute," Jack interrupted. "I remember that song, but it wasn't Gramma singing, it was Dad, and it couldn't have been Irish, because it was about Loch Lomonde in Scotland."

"No doubt our Scottish cousins, nostalgic for their native Erin, appropriated the melody and adapted it for their own purposes. But I understand about Dad and Loch Lomonde. You see," he whispered, "there was a woman."

"A woman?"

"It was during the war, the big one. Dad was stationed in Scotland and he fell in love with a bonnie Scottish lass and they used to go rowing out on Loch Lomonde together, until he got shipped off to France. Then, when the war ended in Europe, he had one week's leave and he went to see her before getting sent back to the states to prepare for the invasion of Japan. They wanted to get married, and would have, but she was a God-fearing Presbyterian and he was a God-fearing Catholic and they tried and tried to figure a way to do it, but things were different then and it just wasn't possible. She needed to promise to bring up their children in the Catholic Church and couldn't. He wanted her like crazy but wouldn't marry outside the Church. Neither one of them could compromise on beliefs they held higher than their own love. So, there was nothing left to be said but goodbye, and that's how we got to be half-Italian instead of half-Scot.

"Sometimes on Sunday mornings when I'm feeling a little tired and want to skip Mass, I think about what Dad gave up so that his kids could be raised in the Faith, and I think about that girl in the rowboat who couldn't understand that stubborn pig-headed loveable American."

Now Neil started, and Jack joined in as twilight settled over the suburbs.

You'll take the high road, and I'll take the low road,
And I'll be in Scotland afore ye,
Where me and my true love will never meet again
On the bonnie bonnie banks of Loch Lomonde.

Chapter 8.

Gold Harbor, Maine

Between his part-time job as an Assistant District Attorney and his full-time job as a sole practitioner, squeezing in a vacation was tough for Jack, but with a baby due in two months and their five year anniversary coming up on Friday, he had long ago decided that this would be a good time to get away, so the next day Jack and Maria and Laura began a less-than-thunder run to Gold Harbor, stopping fairly frequently at the rest areas and for more than an hour at Nubble Light where they took a whole roll of film of Laura in front of the lighthouse, and Laura and Mom, and Laura and Dad, and a couple of crooked ones of Mom and Dad, and finally one of the three of them taken by a passing kind soul.

Jack, though ordinarily somewhat frugal, had splurged on this trip, booking the Gold Harbor Beach Inn months in advance, and a special wink at Sally had guaranteed the romantic second floor suite overlooking the beach and the ocean. Maria had not been there before, and was decidedly impressed with her husband's taste and consideration. Jack particularly liked this suite because it had a separate small bedroom for Laura with her own television.

The first thing Jack and Maria did was drag the gold love seat in front of the sliding door to their private balcony and sat and snuggled and enjoyed. It was already dark by the time they were settled, so Laura went to bed while Mom and Dad stared out at the stars and the sky and the surf and contemplated the mysteries of the universe and after a while contemplated each other, delightfully.

Next morning they all slept late, then, after a couple of hours on the beach looking for shells and digging deep holes and wading in up to their knees (it being the third week of July and the Maine waters finally having warmed to knee-depth tolerability), Maria was ready to shop.

Jack had hated to shop, he thought, but so much enjoyed the uninterrupted company of his family that he was actually beginning to like it. Almost.

A couple of blocks back from the beach were a series antique stores, collectible stores, second-hand stores and junk stores. Maria wanted to tour each one.

Jack strolled along, generally finding something of interest just as his wife was ready to move on to the next place, but theirs was a gentle compromise and things never became unpleasant.

Late in the afternoon Maria called to him from the other end of one recyclable emporium.

"Hey, I found something for your brother!"

It was a neatly preserved copy of a local newspaper, *The Gold Harbor Gazette*, cleverly dated, "Moonday, July 21, 1969". The front page consisted solely of a fuzzy kinescopic wire-photo of the lunar lander with two space-suited figures saluting an American flag. Jack bought it.

As it turns out, that was their only purchase of the day, another reason Jack didn't mind shopping with his wife.

Laura was getting a little cranky, so they stopped for fish and chips, with applesauce and cottage cheese on the side, and a spectacular cup of New England clam chowder.

It had been a full day, so they passed on an evening walk on the beach and settled in early. Laura hopped in bed with her television while Jack and Maria turned on the reading lamps in opposite corners of the main room, Jack with a mystery novel and Maria with their new old newspaper. She was a back-to-front reader and frequently interrupted his train of thought with observations from her reading, but theirs was a gentle compromise and things never became unpleasant.

"Look at this. STAR Market was selling china for seventy-nine cents!"

"Gee, and I thought Manhattan was cheap," Jack muttered.

"That's not very funny."

"Never said it was."

"I hope you don't find this funny: 'Girl, 14, Loses Leg'."

"Sure hope she found it," Jack sputtered, then ducked as the pillow came sailing toward where his head had been but a moment earlier.

But theirs was a gentle compromise and things never became unpleasant, so they met on the love seat, neutral territory, and together reviewed the events of July 1969 A.D.

This time they started from the front. The first four pages, including the photograph-only front page, were devoted exclusively to the news surrounding the moon landing and the limitless future of the space program. The people of Gold Harbor and the rest of the world were blissfully unaware of the grim secret speech President Nixon had been prepared to deliver to the nation in the event the lift-off from the lunar surface failed or some other tragedy developed for the brave astronauts.

The next page surprised Jack. Again a whole page devoted to a single story, this one about Senator Ted Kennedy and a secretary at a place called Chappaquiddick, and the fact that he would likely be charged with leaving the scene of an accident. The girl had drowned.

"I had no idea that was the same weekend," he told his wife. She wasn't into politics and couldn't remember ever having heard about Chappaquiddick, but was rather surprised that after something like that the man could be returned to the Senate. Jack was not surprised.

Then on the local news page, just above the article on the 14-year-old girl losing her leg, "**TRAGEDY STRIKES AREA FAMILY**". "Read it to me," Jack asked.

> *"Tragedy struck an area family on Saturday when 18-year-old Faith Sullivan fell to her death from the dangerous cliffs overlooking the Atlantic at the end of Gold Harbor Beach.*
>
> *"According to police reports, Miss Sullivan, a recent graduate of Bishop McClure High School, was out for a walk with an unnamed companion when she ventured near the edge of the cliffs. A sudden gust of wind caught her off-balance and she was swept over the side, falling nearly two hundred feet to the rocks below. It was several hours before rescue teams were able to recover her body.*
>
> *"Funeral arrangements are incomplete at this time.*
>
> *"Chief of Police Potter Halloran used the occasion to again warn residents of the dangerous nature of the cliffs and to heed the warning signs posted.*
>
> *"The Town Council has added an item to Tuesday night's agenda to deal with the issue. Among the proposals is to provide for a fine for anyone disregarding the warnings."*

"Maybe they should make that retroactive and sue Ms. Sullivan's estate," observed Jack.

"Sounds like a nice Irish-Catholic girl going to a nice Catholic High School. Really a shame. Kids think they're immortal."

"Yeah," Jack said, "Stupid teenagers." And he didn't notice but at 33 that was the very first time that he had denigrated the young, a habit he would soon carry for the rest of his life.

And then he remembered the ring.

"Stay here, babe. I've got to check on something downstairs."

"Hope it's not Sally. She seems a little old for you."

"Nah, she's Bull's girl."

Five minutes later he was back with the Bishop McClure 1969 ring from the case in the lobby. "Take a look at this. See if you can make out the initials."

Maria turned it over in her hands and held it to the light, finally retrieving a small magnifying glass from her purse. "Looks like 'FS'," she said and suddenly dropped it. "Oh, my God! It's hers! Where did you get this?"

So Jack explained the display in the lobby and the scuba divers and the junk and the treasure and the dog tags and the mysteries of the deep, and the mysteries of the junk, and told her about what it was like under water and the security of the womb and those funny looking plants or animals or whatever they are that retreat into themselves whenever something touches them.

"Just put it back where you got it," she said, and he did, for theirs was a gentle compromise and things never became unpleasant.

That same weekend Sheriff Rushmore returned home with a prognosis for a slow but complete recovery, Bull Heimlich pulled a double shift working on a drug investigation, and Acting Sheriff Whelan Oates, having been convinced that remaining with his wife would be foolish, rented an apartment and then spent the next three days at a resort in the Adirondacks happily, hopelessly, goofily in love with Ms. Lynn Reynard.

They talked of marriage and children and what they would name them, and where they would take their vacations together, and where they might live.

"But Whelan, the last thing I need is for people to think that I'm some kind of home-wrecker. Your marriage was on the ropes long before I came around and I do not want to be blamed for it," she worried.

He held her. "You are not the cause. You are the hope," and thought himself the poet of poets for coming up with that one.

She kissed him for the thousandth time.

"Nevertheless, we must keep our relationship secret for now, for my reputation and yours. Can you promise me that?"

"Anything," he groveled.

"So, you get your divorce right away, and then maybe after a year or so we can start being seen in public together. Till then, we'll see each other all the time and sometimes you can come to my place and sometimes we'll be at your place and sometimes we'll just get away like this," she said, smiling her entrancing smile, focusing those magnificent eyes, and grabbing him and hauling him back under the sheets.

In Cotton Falls, New York Patty Hartwick's sister pulled out a box of the

-58-

personal belongings of the deceased and started thumbing through them. What a wasted life, she thought, always living on the far edge, the drugs, the alcohol, the strange men, the mental breakdowns.

She lifted a spiral notebook and examined its contents. Poetry. Well, of a sort, she thought. None of it seems to rhyme, though I guess that's not necessary any more. Most of it was incomprehensible, though the references to Marge and Daisy were explicit enough. Quite explicit.

She's suffered enough in life. I'm not going to let her suffer more in death, decided the sister as she carefully tore out the pages and crumbled them in the fireplace and, in spite of the 85 degree temperature, incinerated them.

Chapter 9.

On Thursday a kiddy carnival opened in Gold Harbor and Maria, suspecting that Jack would not make attendance his first choice, suggested that he find a way to keep himself busy for a few hours while mom and Laura did kid things. Jack thoroughly appreciated the gesture and the opportunity to shop for an anniversary present a whole day in advance.

They had spoken no more of Faith Sullivan, but Jack felt a nagging duty to do something about the ring, so he found the local library and the microfilm records of the *Gold Harbor Gazette* for the last seventy-eight years.

The paper came out twice weekly, that being reasonably sufficient most times for catching up on events in the town. The July 24, 1969 edition contained a complete obituary for Faith Sullivan, listing parents and relatives and the arrangements for the funeral which had already passed by the time the paper hit the streets.

Armed with that information and an address from the phone book and the ring from the Inn, Jack was soon knocking on the door of Michael and Genevieve Sullivan.

"Mrs. Sullivan?" She nodded. "My name is Jack Hughes and you don't know me. I'm just a tourist here, but if you are the mother of Faith Sullivan, I think I have something that you should have." And he handed her the ring (which he had cleaned up as much as possible) and the seventy-five-year-old woman caught a sob in her throat and quickly invited Jack in, calling for her husband at the same time.

"How? Where?" She choked out. Jack helped her sit down and introduced himself to Michael Sullivan, a big man with a great deal of wear on his face.

So Jack carefully recounted the story and the coincidences which had helped him solve this little mystery and return the treasure to its rightful owner.

"I can't believe you would go to all this trouble for somebody you don't even know!" she marveled. "You must be an angel. God sent you to us."

"Didn't have any wings, last I checked," laughed Jack, "and if there's a halo hanging over me, I suspect it's a bit on the tarnished side.

"You are an angel," she affirmed nonetheless and was soon busy in the kitchen preparing a snack while Michael Sullivan grabbed a beer for himself and his young friend.

"Every year this time, it's hard for us," Michael said wistfully. "It was thirty years this week. Well, you know that," and he grew quiet. Genevieve placed a tray with food for an army in front of Jack and he politely partook.

"Tell me," he said between bites, "if it's not too hard for you. Tell me about your daughter. Until now for me she's only been a name in a newspaper or initials on a ring. Tell me what she was like."

And now out come the scrapbooks and the yearbooks and the photo albums and the 11x14 senior picture from the wall. And now Jack began to glimpse the vivacious, fun-loving, thoroughly attractive young girl as she passed from booties to sneakers to ballet shoes to high heels. He sees her grow up before his eyes: the violinist, the drama club ingenue, the cheerleader, the homecoming queen. And he holds that senior picture of a girl forever young, with the medium length blond hair and the sparkling, entrancing green eyes (even in a photograph) and he sees not death, but life.

She reminded him a little of Lynn.

CLANG CLANG CLANG.

Ms. Reynard, he corrected himself but still gets another CLANG for his troubles.

"Her thirtieth high school reunion is coming up this year, the Saturday after Thanksgiving," Genevieve remarked. "Those kids are so good. They always remember us and invite us. We've never been, but maybe this year we will go. They always mention the ones who have gone, and even set a table for them. . .Well."

With that, Jack knew it was time to go and to leave them to their memories, and part of him is sorry that he has rekindled their grief, but remembering now the deaths of his parents he observes that grief isn't such a bad thing in and of itself. It is, after all, a reflection of that part of love which is eternal and transcends the grave. Far better to be wept over than forgotten.

Genevieve insisted on getting Jack's address so she could send him a proper thank-you, and hugged him, as did Big Mike.

On his way to pick up his family at the carnival, Jack found a most appropriate anniversary present for his lovely wife, and the next day when she received it, she was most appreciative, and showed him her appreciation later, when Laura was asleep and the world was still.

"You know," he said finally, "I really like you."

"And I really, really, really like you, John Robert Hughes, Sr." and she showed him she really meant it this time, in case there had ever been a question.

August in DeWitt County Court was spent dealing with the usual pre-trial motions and hearings in the Nichols case. Ms. Reynard demanded any and all exculpatory material in the possession of the People, which the People perfunctorily stated did not exist, but would be supplied immediately should it come to their attention. The defendant attempted to suppress the search of her apartment, which after a hearing at which Jack and Bull testified, was denied.

Ms. Reynard asked the Court to examine the transcript of the Grand Jury proceedings and determine that the indictment should be dismissed for legal insufficiency, also denied. She was permitted to examine and have scientifically tested certain items of physical evidence, and given copies of all the photographs taken by the People.

She requested a ruling by the Court that Martin Kilhooey was an Accomplice, as that term is defined by the Criminal Procedure Law, as a Matter of Law. That also became the subject of a hearing at which Martin and Daisy both testified, and in due course the Court determined that the issue of whether Martin was an Accomplice was a question of fact for the jury to decide.

Finally, the defendant having given notice of intention to present evidence to show that she was NOT GUILTY by reason of mental disease or defect, partly on the basis of the letter from Daisy's first grade teacher, permission was granted to have the defendant examined by a psychiatrist at public expense with the results to be shared with the People, and the People were likewise given the opportunity to arrange for their own examination.

"So, Jack, old buddy, I like what you did for those old folks back in Gold Harbor. That was pretty good detective work and a very nice thing to do. Almost sounds like something *I'd* do," said Bull after one of the hearings.

"Well, it may *sound* like something you *might* do, but the fact remains that *I* solved the mystery and *I* returned the ring," bragged Jack.

"Yeah, yeah. Too bad, though."

"What's too bad?"

"That you didn't solve the *whole* mystery," Bull noted.

"What do you mean?" Jack asked warily.

"Well, you didn't, for example, find out who murdered her, and why."

"She wasn't murdered, Bull. She fell off a cliff."

Bull got quiet. "Says who, Jack?"

"Says, says . . . I don't know. That's what it said in the paper!" Jack was getting frustrated and now a little nagging doubt was starting to bug him, even though he knew Bull was just doing this because he was jealous and didn't really mean anything by it.

"Who, Jack?"

"I guess, I guess it was whoever was with her," and now the nag got louder.

"And that person was?"

"That person was . . . *'an unnamed companion'*," quoted Jack.

"An unnamed companion. You know what, Jack, I'm almost willing to bet that Faith Sullivan's unnamed companion had a name. Maybe *has* a name, even."

"You know, Bull, you can really be a jerk sometimes."

"I've heard that."

But a Thunder Run was out of the question for now, what with Maria so close to her due date. Jack suspected just a little that if he accidentally missed the birth of his child, the compromise could possibly get a little less gentle and the risk of things becoming unpleasant might increase somewhat for a time.

So he stayed near home, getting a bit domestic, even, and for the next few weeks worked on doing over one of the bedrooms for the new baby, even painting it blue, because he remembered that Maria had called him "John Robert Hughes, Sr." when they were celebrating their anniversary and he figured women have some sort of magical way of knowing these things, even when there had been no scientific testing done.

Accordingly he was not at all surprised when his wife gave birth to a healthy, nearly nine pound baby boy on September 13, 1999. He was, however, surprised that the sight of a little bit of blood with the birth made him woozy. God knows, if there had been any mayonnaise or strawberry jam present he might have fainted dead away.

As was becoming his tradition, after cutting the cord he gave his son his first bath.

"Welcome to the world, John Robert Hughes, Jr. It's time you began to learn the songs of you ancestors, as your father did and his father before him." And before long Baby Jack was hearing all about gypsy rovers and wearing green and hanging people on bridges and wild colonial boys, and that haunting melody of Scotland's Loch Lomonde which in Ireland was also, remarkably, about lost love.

> *'Twas down near Killarney's green woods that we strayed;*
> *The moon and the stars they were shining;*
> *The moon shone her rays on her locks of golden hair,*
> *And she swore she'd be my love forever.*

Chapter 10.

Lynn Reynard reviewed the psychiatric report and was not pleased. *What the heck do we pay these guys for? You put your client through all this emotional torture just to establish proof that she lacked the capacity to form an intent for the heinous crime charged and then all they can come up with is a diagnosis of some vague-sounding personality disorders.* Conclusion: Daisy Nichols may have some issues, but she was perfectly capable of committing murder.

Lynn didn't have much use for psychiatrists, especially after those two months she had spent under the watchful eye of one at that country hospital when she had been overcome by the stress of her marriage breakup and her mother's early death and that awful confrontation with her brother. Only thing worse than a psychiatrist was a country yahoo psychiatrist. If he knew what he was doing, what the hell would he be doing there?

I know myself pretty darn well, she had told him, *and a lot longer than you have, and I think that if I was suffering from Narcissistic Personality Disorder or Borderline Personality Disorder, or any other freakin' disorder it would have come to my attention long before this. And that sexual abuse when I was a kid, I've dealt with that in my own way, and I'm a much stronger person for it. How can anyone say I'm not sympathetic to other people's pain? I've spent all these years in social work. That has to count for something. And what was that stupid "inability to form lasting relationships"? Christ, I was married for four years, not exactly a drop in the bucket.* And when he reminded her that she had stopped having sex with her husband after two years, and that might, just might, have had something to do with that old sexual abuse, she said *that's it*, declared herself cured and checked herself out.

For the next three years she'd buried herself in the study of the law, switching careers and switching towns and leaving her stupid past behind her. *No use hanging out with those hicks, anyway. They wouldn't know talent if it was staring at them.* She should have been Deputy Commissioner before she left, and would have been, too, if it hadn't been for that petty jealousy and those small-town, small-minded busybodies who kept spreading those stories about her and the married social services attorney.

As if she'd waste a relationship on him, him with the linguini spine who couldn't stand up to his wife and kept running back to her.

A man for me needs to have more character than that.

And it sure isn't Whelan. God, he's getting boring. Maybe Jack Hughes. He'd be a challenge. A little pudge round the middle, maybe, but I could convince him to start working out. Men do things like that for me. And his wife, just having a baby, he'd probably be ready for some action. I like the way Judge Blaine looks at me. There's a guy who can appreciate class when he sees it, I'll bet. Bull might be good for a night or two, no commitments.

But, it was love she was looking for. Hopeless, delirious, everlasting love and a home and a dog and a pool and kids, maybe.

Why can't I just have what everybody else has? Is that too much to ask?

"OK, Jack, old buddy, you asked me to find out about Ms. Reynard, and I am ready to report, if you're up for it," said Bull as he plopped himself into a chair at the Law Office of John. R. Hughes.

"Shoot."

"The line on her is that she just wants what everybody else has," Bull replied.

"Meaning?"

"Meaning that if any woman has a husband or boyfriend, she wants him for herself."

Jack whistled. "And when she catches them?"

Debbie Budoniak, faithful secretary, interrupted. "She tosses them in a pile until their carcasses rot and when the stench finally becomes overwhelming she moves on."

"You know her?" Jack asked.

"I know her type," said Debbie. "Boy, do I know her type!"

Jack turned to Bull. "So how does knowing this help us at trial?"

"It don't. But let me tell ya, Jack, when your marriage vows start to bend, this little bit of knowledge might be just the extra boost you need to bounce back," Bull advised.

Jack smiled. "Strange advice from the author of the Heimlich Maneuver."

"Good advice, Jack. Good advice. . .

"So, Debbie, whatcha doin' for lunch?"

On the First Monday of October, the Supreme Court of the United States commenced its annual term and in DeWitt County Court jury selection began in the case of *The People of the State of New York vs. Daisy Nichols*, Judge Samuel R. Blaine presiding.

Unlike television and movie trials, even murder trials in DeWitt County rarely draw a crowd. Building employees would occasionally stop by, the District Attorney's father liked to watch his son in action, two of the defendant's siblings would drop in almost every day and otherwise the big old ornate 19th century courtroom was pretty much empty for the duration of the trial. Even press coverage was limited to one reporter from a regional newspaper who watched most of the action, and one other reporter who dropped by late every afternoon to get an update from the District Attorney.

From the moment the District Attorney had arrived on the scene back in March, Jack Hughes had been frozen out of the prosecution and preparation of the case, with the brief exception of the felony hearing early on, and even then he was only backing up Bull. He was being treated as an ordinary witness and would have had no idea of the District Attorney's strategy in the case, but for the fact that he knew the District Attorney and his strategy was always the same.

Some prosecutors like to start with a bang and end with a bang, presenting evidence to a jury in a way most likely to keep their attention and impress them. Hit them early on with the gruesomeness of the crime itself, close with your most compelling evidence of the defendant's guilt.

The District Attorney of DeWitt County, on the other hand, belonged to the linear school. Nothing flamboyant, nothing dramatic, just a steady unraveling of the story in chronological order. Depending on the nature of the evidence, it might be the third or fourth day of the trial before the victim showed up dead, and the trial might well close with the last lab technician reporting on his analysis of the last nearly-insignificant piece of physical evidence.

He also believed in the *Star Trek, the Motion Picture* method of presentation, meaning that if you spent money and effort producing something, you must include it in the final product, even though judicious editing might make it more entertaining and/or comprehensible. Thus, every last piece of broken glass, every emptied ashtray, every everything would be submitted in evidence. Once, in a shooting case, he had the whole plaster wall severed from the house and brought to court so the jury could see the bullet holes for themselves.

His examination of witnesses was similarly methodical and plodding, every single question and probable answer written out in advance on endless sheets of yellow legal paper and if, as witnesses often do, a witness jumped off the track and started anticipating answers to future questions, the District Attorney would stop, and then carefully guide the witness back to the place on the track where the witness had jumped off. If necessary, questions would be repeated several times until they were finally at the same point on the straight line to Conviction.

-67-

It reminded Jack somewhat of the game of Chutes and Ladders.

This method took time, but it was thorough, and, judging by his conviction record, successful. Fact is that most jurors take their jobs seriously and know they are not there to be entertained, but to determine the truth. When he was done, no one could say they wanted to hear more, because by then they had heard it all. This approach might not work everywhere, but in the small yeoman counties of upstate New York, jurors generally seemed to appreciate the straight-forward no-nonsense approach.

A defense attorney's job was much different. Chip away at the edges of the People's witnesses, with an occasional thrust at the heart. If lucky, which happened rarely, you might connect and blow the case out of the water. Usually, however, you look to pile up REASONABLE DOUBT, the defense attorney's best friend. Defense attorneys always say "Reasonable Doubt" as though it were all one word, a concept etched in granite, while prosecutors inevitably emphasize two separated words, with the primary emphasis being on *reasonable.*

Lynn Reynard may not have tried many cases, but she was smart and quick on her feet. She had a game plan, and the plan was two-pronged, first to convince the jury that Martin Kilhooey was an accomplice, so that his testimony would need to be corroborated, and secondly to show that enough suspicion existed to believe that Martin himself might have committed the murder, at least a strong enough possibility to create REASONABLE DOUBT.

Ms. Reynard was in something of a quandary. She had spent endless hours interviewing her client, read all the reports then available to her, reviewed the oral statements purportedly made, sat through all the pretrial hearings; she had squeezed more than a little inside information from Whelan Oates, and yet still felt that she had not gotten the whole story, particularly from Daisy. It is very difficult to prepare a defense if your own client is holding out on you. Makes it hard to defend against surprises. Lynn Reynard did not like to be surprised.

While she assumed Daisy was guilty of the crimes charged, and geared her defense strategy accordingly, with all these odd witnesses and an odd victim and an odd defendant, anything was possible, and there just might be enough confusion to make some of the jurors think twice.

In any event, THE LAW presumed Daisy Nichols innocent and it was up to The People to prove the contrary, which they began to do on Wednesday, October 6, 1999 at 9:30 a.m.

"The People call as their first witness Marjory Brown," announced the District Attorney after preliminary instructions to the jury and opening statements by the attorneys.

In his linear presentation, the District Attorney reserved the right to call this witness twice, first to establish what happened early that Saturday evening, then much later to discuss the events following the arrival of Daisy Nichols on her doorstep after she had jumped from the ambulance.

Marge was all business. The District Attorney liked that kind of witness, as she methodically described the store, the apartment building, her son's apartment next door, the street, the alley, the roof, the tenants. She identified photographs of the scenes, floor plans of the apartments, even recalled having seen Daisy Nichols on prior occasions with a knife similar to the one shown her as People's Exhibit One for identification.

Then she went on to describe the personalities of the tenants, the length of their tenancies, the way they interrelated. Then when asked about the evening of March 27, 1999 she recalled the argument between Daisy and Patty Hartwick, how upset Daisy had been about Patty quitting her job, how Patty had gone upstairs and how Martin and Daisy had left shortly after, and how she had closed the store and gone home across the river.

"No further questions at this time," concluded the District Attorney.

"Cross examination, Miss Reynard?"

"Thank you, your honor," smiled Attorney Reynard.

"Now is it Miss, Mrs., or Ms. Brown?"

"It's Mrs., but you can call me Ms., I guess. Haven't seen my husband in fifteen years." The jury tittered. As a rule, prosecutors do not like tittering juries in murder cases.

"Now, Ms. Brown," continued the defense attorney, "you stated in direct testimony that you have known Martin Kilhooey as a tenant for some two and a half years. Did you know him before that?"

"Yes. I've known him from hanging around the store for maybe seven or eight years, and I knew *of* him before that."

"You say you knew '*of* him'. Does that mean that from time to time you have heard other people talk about him?" she inquired.

"Yes."

"And say, over the last five years, have you had an opportunity to learn of Martin Kilhooey's reputation in the community for truthfulness?"

"You mean whether he tells the truth?"

"Yes, whether he has a reputation for telling the truth," Lynn explained.

"I guess I have heard of his reputation."

"And what is that reputation?"

"OBJECTION!" shouted the District Attorney.

"I can hear you quite well in a normal tone of voice, sir," admonished

Judge Blaine. "Your objection is overruled. The witness may answer the question."

"Exception," said the District Attorney in a normal tone of voice.

Now the Judge turned back in his direction. "Need I remind The People that the requirement to say 'exception' after an adverse ruling was abolished by the legislature of this state back when you were in elementary school?" The jury tittered again and this time the District Attorney *really* did not like a tittering jury as his face reddened.

By this time the witness had completely forgotten the question, so it was read back by the court reporter.

"Yeah, I know Martin's reputation. I don't know anyone who would believe a word he says."

"OBJECTION."

"Overruled."

And just as "Exception" was about to escape his lips, the District Attorney caught it and sat down.

"And Ms. Brown, you've told us that Daisy was upset that Patty had quit her job, is that right?"

"Right."

"Now Daisy isn't the only person who thought that Patty was stupid to quit her job, was she?" Ms. Reynard asked.

"What do you mean?"

"Well, didn't Martin also say in your presence that *he* thought it was stupid for Miss Hartwick to quit her job?"

Marge nodded. "Yes, as a matter of fact, he did!"

"And you yourself thought it was pretty stupid, didn't you?"

"I guess I did," Marge agreed.

"But just because you thought Patty Hartwick was being stupid doesn't mean you felt like killing her, does it?"

"Nope. Wouldn't kill her just because she was stupid," Marge noted.

"In fact, if people were being killed just for being stupid, there'd be a whole lot fewer people in the world, wouldn't there?"

"Objection."

"Sustained."

"Probably be fewer people in this courtroom," Marge answered anyway, and the jury tittered.

Chapter 11.

After Ms. Brown's testimony, the District Attorney decided to veer away from his straight line just a little and moved Martin Kilhooey much, much further down the witness list. Better play it safe for now.

Marie Daley was a little flighty, but she was the only witness who could lay an admission on the defendant, so she told her story. The jury paid close attention to the testimony about Daisy and the door knob, and Daisy smashing Patty on the side of her head, causing blood to spill, and Daisy and the knife. Especially Daisy and the knife.

"I show you People's Exhibit One for identification. Have you seen this knife before?"

"Yes. That's the knife Daisy showed me at my house that night."

"And when you say that night, are you referring to the night of March 27/28, 1999?"

"Yes."

"Your honor, the People offer Exhibit One in evidence."

The District Attorney handed the knife and sheath to Attorney Reynard.

"*Voir dire* of the witness, Miss Reynard?" asked the Judge.

"Thank you. Mrs. Daley, this looks like a pretty ordinary hunting knife. How can you be sure this is the same knife you saw one night for a few moments over six months ago?" reasoned Ms. Reynard.

"That's easy. I sold her the knife. It used to be mine. Has a nick on the handle where I dropped it once," and the witness pointed to the nick on the handle as Attorney Reynard quickly sat down muttering "No objection."

The District Attorney continued his examination. "Do you recall whether the defendant, Daisy Nichols, said anything that evening about Martin Kilhooey?"

"Yes. She said that he'd better not say anything about what happened to Patty or she'd kill him or take care of him, I'm not sure which she said."

"Objection," said Ms. Reynard, politely.

"Sustained. Mrs. Daley," said the judge, "you can't just guess as to what was said. Take your time and think and then tell us to the best of your recollection what the defendant said that night, and if you're not sure, then be honest and just tell us you're not sure."

Marie Daley thought long and hard. "I'm not sure," she said, finally.

"The Jury will disregard the comments made by the witness about what the defendant said about Martin Kilhooey. Strike it from your mind as though it never happened. You are not to consider the question or answer in any way," instructed the judge.

On cross examination, Ms. Reynard guided the witness to emphasizing that Daisy had never admitted stabbing anyone, hadn't been exactly crystal clear about whether she or Martin had removed the doorknob and had mentioned that Martin had been with Daisy when they entered the Hartwick apartment.

"Now, you know all the people involved here. Do you know whether it would have been unusual for residents of that building to walk in on each other?"

"Heck, no. Doors were always open. Any one of them would be as likely as not to pop in on another any time of the day or night. It was like one big family, and my mom was the mother hen."

Just a typical American family thought the District Attorney and shuddered.

That night Whelan Oates called Lynn at home.

"Whelan, you know I love you, but we really have to avoid each other while this trial is going on. Somebody might be watching," Lynn warned.

"Hey, I'm in charge. I'd know if anybody was watching!"

"I don't care. I'm nervous about the whole thing. Please try and understand and I'll make it up to you when the trial's over, ok? I mean I'll *really* make it up to you," she oozed.

And of course he believed her.

Meanwhile, at the Rushmore home where Bull had stopped in for a visit, as he had been doing regularly, the sheriff was apologizing.

"Bull, I know he's made a mess of things, but right now, there's just nothing I can do. I just can't go back to work yet," and he winced as he shifted in his chair, "but I promise you, things will be different when I get back."

"It's all right boss. I've lived through worse things than Whelan Oates," said Bull. "Anyway, I didn't come here to complain, but to pick your brain. Got a couple of minutes?"

"That's all it'll take to pick what's left of my brain, I'm afraid," said Rushmore. They both chuckled.

"Now I know Patty Hartwick was a bit of a flake and a little drunk, but don't you think somebody who'd been hit hard enough to bleed and had her chest swiped with a hunting knife would have called for help? We know her phone was working, we used it ourselves. She had plenty of time to call for help after Daisy left the first time. Why didn't she?" Bull asked.

"Why she didn't, I can't say, but she must not have called anybody, otherwise Whelan would have mentioned it," the sheriff replied.

"Whelan? Why Whelan?"

"Because I specifically asked him to check with the phone company just before I went out to talk to that ambulance driver. Had I not been delayed on the return trip," he paused and reviewed his battered body, then continued, "I would have expected those results within the hour. As you know, we have very good relations with the local phone company."

Bull didn't have the heart to tell the Sheriff that his trusted Undersheriff had screwed up, that there was no record anywhere in the file that Whelan Oates had ever made that simple call, nor that he had asked anyone else to do so.

Thursday and Friday the other lay witnesses testified, Andy and Christy and Carl, Jr and cousin Steve, all telling about the finding of the nearly dead body, none showing any obvious hostility to the defendant, each testifying when asked that Martin Kilhooey's reputation for telling the truth wasn't very good.

Attorney Reynard was particularly interested in Andrew Brown's testimony about finding Martin in the alley after retrieving the sheet to cover the victim.

"Now where exactly does that alley lead?" she asked, and he told about the way you could get on to the garage roof and from there to the roof over the store and from there to Daisy's apartment or the second floor hallway.

"So, I take it, the reverse is also possible, that you could exit the apartment or the hallway and escape fairly easily to the alley?"

"Oh, sure. I've done it lots of times."

"Now there's been some indication that Martin Kilhooey had a brace on his leg that evening, and I take it you saw that?"

"Yes, I did."

"And how was he walking with the brace on his leg?" she asked.

"Seemed perfectly normal to me, other than he was keeping the leg straight. He didn't use any crutches or anything."

"And was there anything, anything at all that you observed about Daisy Nichols that evening that would cause you to believe that she might have committed this murder?"

"Nope. Can't think of anything."

The District Attorney didn't want the jury disbanding for the long holiday weekend without something at least a little incriminating, so the ambulance people took the stand, and in the context of the nature of the case, and coming right after the "cover her with a sheet" testimony, having Daisy trying to jump in the back of the ambulance with the victim, then jumping out and running away seemed peculiar, but as Ms. Reynard correctly elicited on cross-examination, many, many people try to ride in the back with a patient. It's only natural, they agreed, that if two people were close the healthy one would want to be right there for the hurting one.

But "Polly Eckler" was a bit more difficult to explain, and after the ambulance driver told how Daisy had given that phony name at the hospital and identified the paper handed him by the defendant, Ms. Reynard made no effort to explain it away at all with that witness, and the jury was left to chew on that till Tuesday, although they were sternly admonished by Judge Blaine not to form any conclusions at all at this time and have a nice weekend.

Night after night Whelan Oates returned to his lonely apartment. Night after night he resisted the temptation to pick up the telephone and call her. She had been very clear about that. He thought about his wife and their ten-year-old daughter and wondered if he would ever see them again. In the aftermath of the breakup they had moved to North Carolina and their home, which technically was owned by his wife's parents, was on the market. So he went in to the office more often, checked up on the third shift guys once in a while, drove the lonely roads at night, and occasionally stopped for a beer here and there.

By Monday night he couldn't stand it any more, so he decided to drive over to Bath Springs to that cozy bar that she had called "Our Place" because no one knew them and they could relax with each other. Maybe, just maybe, she'd get lonely tonight, too. It had to have been as bad for her as it was for him. Had to be. They were like two teenagers in love, she had kept saying over and over, and it was true, he supposed, though he hadn't had that much luck as a teenager himself.

Her car was there and his heart skipped a beat. He lingered at the door, not wanting to do the wrong thing, wanting to make his appearance look casual and uncontrived.

He looked through the window and saw her.

There was nothing about her that looked contrived or uncasual.

She was draped over the pool table with a big scuzzy-looking biker leaning over her, helping her with her shot, and she was giggling away and then they were face to face and laughing and then he was placing his fat slimy lips all over her and she was licking his face including that thickly encrusted beard and his hands were all over her and her hands were all over him and in a moment Whelan was all over both of them and the fists started flying and the bottles started breaking and Lynn started screaming, "WHELAN! WHAT THE FUCK ARE YOU DOING!" but Whelan heard nothing and just kept on punching and punching and punching and being punched till four men from the Gates County Sheriff's Department grabbed him and drove him away battered, bruised and bloody.

The biker departed under his own power, dignity and cocaine intact, and Lynn Reynard just stood in the middle of the room screaming hysterically until the bartender put his arm around her and consoled her and comforted her and took her to his bed.

Early the next morning she thanked him, in a very special way, then returned to her apartment, prepared herself for the day, and arrived at the DeWitt County Courthouse at 9:30 a.m. ready to joust with the next witness.

Chapter 12.

When the District Attorney had learned of the events of the previous evening, he assigned Jack Hughes to find out from Whelan what the hell was going on. The Sheriff had ordered his own investigation and suspended his Undersheriff with pay, but the District Attorney didn't like the smell of things and needed to know how any of this would affect the outcome of the trial.

Undersheriff Oates was sitting up in his hospital bed. Jack barely recognized Whelan through the swelling.

"Ouch!" he said.

"Big ouch," Whelan replied, attempting to smile.

"Was it worth it?"

And suddenly Whelan began to cry. The whole reservoir had been building up overnight, maybe for a whole week, and he'd been fighting it off, but now it just let loose and it wouldn't stop and Jack listened to those great, heaving, agonizing sobs and watched his whole body break out in tremors. At first he hid his face in his hands, but then he dropped them and just looked plaintively at Jack, tears streaming down his face.

"I've lost it all, Jack. I've lost it all."

And so he poured out his soul, and Jack heard more than he need to know about the problems in Whelan's marriage that made him so . . .vulnerable. And then Whelan described the first time he laid eyes on Ms. Reynard (and Jack recalled the CLANGCLANGCLANG and wondered if Whelan had been similarly blessed, but decided he hadn't), and then that first beer together and the way she had looked at him and the things she had said and the realization that this beautiful, charming, smart, talented wonderful woman had fallen in love with him, him, Whelan Oates, a guy most women never pay attention to, and then the whirlwind romance, things that happened so fast that he couldn't even believe it talking about it now, and the way they talked about marriage and kids and where they would live and take their vacations, and how they were like two teenagers in love for the first time, and the things that she would do with her body, Jack, and with me and oh, God, while it lasted I never felt so wonderful and so . . .ALIVE! That's it, Jack, she made me feel like I was alive for the first time in my life, thirty-five years of numbing existence changed overnight, and I knew, I just knew, Jack, that this is the way it's supposed to be and she loved me, Jack, she loved me and I loved her and nothing else in the whole world mattered and when she worried about how people might call her a home wrecker, I told her, Jack, I told her, I said *You are not the Cause, you are the HOPE* and she was, Jack, she was. . .she was all I had ever hoped for and dreamed of my entire life, and now . . ."

"And now," said Bull Heimlich who had entered the hospital room, "you know that none of it was ever real at all and you wasted all your affection on someone who never existed and you feel like a first class schmuck, is that it, Whelan?"

"Yeah," he said quietly. "That's it exactly, Bull."

"Well, guess what, Whelan, you ain't the first guy this has ever happened to and you won't be the last because that's just the way some women are and you're lucky it hasn't happened to you a dozen times already. So quit feeling sorry for yourself, pick yourself up and start living the rest of your life."

"It's easy for you, Bull, you haven't lost it all."

"Yeah, well lemme tell ya, I've done a few things in my life that I'm not proud of, and I've gotten myself into stupid situations and I know what it's like to follow the little general blindly into places you don't belong, and I've caused some pain to my wife and my kids and I know it and I wish I could go back and change some things, but you know what, Whelan? You can't. So you just muddle through the best you can and hope you can make up for some of it, and if you can't, well, that's that, and you try to learn from your mistakes, and even if you keep making them, at least some good can come out of it if you can convince even one person 'Don't do what I did', and that's all you can do, Whelan, because you know what? THAT'S LIFE."

Whelan looked up at his oft-antagonist and said, sincerely, "Thanks, Bull. Thanks a lot."

"Yeah, well, you're welcome. Just don't kiss me."

"No problem."

Jack cleared his throat. "Ah, Whelan, I was actually sent here by the District Attorney for a specific purpose, and it may be a little touchy, I understand, but we really need to know . . . how much did you tell her about the Nichols case?"

Whelan sighed. "Everything, Jack. Everything."

A week and a day after jury selection had begun, Patty Hartwick at last was dead, as firmly established by the testimony of the emergency room doctor and the uncontested admission into evidence of the death certificate. The doctor's description of the wounds was particularly graphic and if the jury hadn't already been convinced that something horrible had happened here, the next witness, the Medical Examiner, put all doubts to rest.

And now, over lunch, the District Attorney faced a crucial decision. Should he call the not-too-reliable Martin Kilhooey and get it over with, or should he play it safe and recall Marge Brown. He considered the fact that Ms. Reynard had not been her usual collected self this morning, and no doubt that little domestic dispute had something to do with that. Maybe this would be the best time to try to slip Martin past her.

On the other hand, it had been like pulling teeth at the Grand Jury to get him to repeat the same story he had told Barney Jackson rather than the new one he had told Bull and Jack during the felony hearing.

On the other hand, he *had* stuck to the original story and odds were he would again, and if he balked, the District Attorney could always use his grand jury testimony to refresh his recollection and subtly remind him of the dangers of a perjury charge in a murder case.

On the other hand, *subtle* is not something which would have much effect on this lamebrain, so maybe he needed to be reminded explicitly by Bull one more time before taking the stand.

Ah, what the heck. Now or never. Let's do it.

The decision made, the District Attorney finished his tuna sub in peace.

"The People call Martin Kilhooey to the stand," and Martin Kilhooey, being duly sworn, began to tell his story, or one of them.

Examining Martin Kilhooey was not easy. First, all the carefully prepared questions on the endless sheets of yellow legal paper need to be translated into a subset of the English language that would be comprehensible to the witness, or rather *so he will know what we are talking about*, thought the District Attorney. Then, he had to draw out the answers out in such a way that Martin's caginess and natural propensity to lie would not be so obvious to the jurors.

But all things considered, it did not go badly. Once again, he was there for the argument in the store, and the yelling upstairs, and the mayonnaise and the strawberry jam, and he watched while Daisy pulled off the doorknob and *saw* Daisy punch out Patty and the blood from that and the thing with the knife and Daisy threatening Patty and telling her she'd better get out.

And most importantly he remembered after 1 a.m. when the ghastly figure of Patty Hartwick dragged herself out of her apartment and tumbled down the stairs and how Daisy came out a little later and how Daisy came up with the story about how they were out walking and couldn't open the door. He said how he didn't tell everything at first because he was scared of Daisy and knew she had a knife and after seeing what happened to Patty, he didn't want any trouble.

"Now, you say you never heard Daisy go up the stairs to Patty's apartment after one o'clock?"

"Right. I was sleeping on Daisy's couch, so I really didn't hear anything. I guess the tv must've been on. Once there was all that noise in the upstairs hall, that's what must've woke me up."

"But there's no question Daisy came down the stairs."

"Right."

"Was she carrying a knife?"

"OBJECTION. Leading and suggestive," noted Ms. Reynard correctly.

"SUSTAINED," the Judge ruled correctly.

"Did you notice whether she was carrying anything?" tried the District Attorney again.

"No, I didn't notice."

"No further questions." The District Attorney sat down.

Lynn Reynard stood and sized up the witness. "Good afternoon, Mr. Kilhooey. My name is Lynn Reynard and I'm representing Daisy Nichols. Should I call you Mr. Kilhooey?" she sparkled.

"Call me whatever you want. Just call me!" and the men on the jury tittered and the women suppressed a titter and the District Attorney grimaced and Judge Blaine smiled at Ms. Reynard who smiled back.

"Now, Martin," she began familiarly, and he liked that, "you told us what happened and those were your own words, right? Nobody told you what to say?"

"Well, other than the District Attorney, no."

"Oh!" exclaimed Lynn, spotting an opening. "And just what did the District Attorney tell you to say?"

"He just said to make sure everything I said was the same as at the Grand Jury."

"And the story you told at the Grand Jury, was that pretty much the same as the one you told here today?"

"Yeah, I think so."

"Now there was a time when you told a different story, wasn't there?"

"Whadya mean?"

"I mean," said Ms. Reynard, "didn't you tell a different story to Investigator Bull Heimlich and Assistant District Attorney Hughes on the night of the felony hearing?" and now the District Attorney turned rigid.

"Yeah, I guess I did."

-80-

"And what story did you tell them that night?"

Martin puzzled over the question, then replied, "I think I told them that I didn't see anything the second time because I was in my own apartment taking a crap." The jury did not titter. They were sitting alertly. Very alertly.

"So you told the investigator and the Assistant District Attorney that you never saw Daisy in the apartment building after 1 a.m., is that right?"

"Yeah, that's what I told them."

"Your honor," said Ms. Reynard, "I believe we need to have a conference outside the presence of the jury."

The jury was excused.

"Your honor," began Attorney Reynard, "the People are required under *Brady* to provide the defense with all exculpatory matter within their knowledge. It seems to me that a prior inconsistent oral statement of the principal witness against the defendant is about as exculpatory as you can get. They failed to so notify me, the defendant is prejudiced, and the only appropriate remedy is to strike the testimony of the witness."

The District Attorney was outraged. "Your honor, first of all I disagree that this is exculpatory matter within the meaning of *Brady*. Second, the only basis for making this claim is the testimony here today of Martin Kilhooey, a man the defense counsel has been trying to prove to be a liar throughout this trial. She can't have it both ways. Finally, there is no prejudice to the defendant since she clearly knew about it anyway, if it happened, and therefore no remedy is necessary or appropriate."

The Judge was livid. "First of all, this allegation, if true, is a very serious matter and involves a breach of professional responsibility on the part of the District Attorney, a violation of the laws and of the constitutional rights of the defendant to a fair and impartial trial. As for the remedy, I don't know what that should be, yet. But I know what I am going to do now. I am directing that the court officers segregate Assistant District Attorney Hughes and Investigator Heimlich immediately. Next, we are going to suspend the order of this trial and we will have an immediate examination of Mr. Hughes and Mr. Heimlich. And, because of the incredibly serious nature of this matter, I am directing that this examination be conducted in the presence of the jury."

"Your honor, I strenuously object!" said the District Attorney in vain.

"Objection duly noted and overruled. Bring the jury back, and bring in Assistant District Attorney Hughes."

Jack was totally bewildered. He hadn't expected to be called as a witness for several days. While he was familiar with his proposed testimony, no one had yet reviewed it with him. After being duly sworn, he was surprised that the District Attorney remained seated. Then he looked over to the defense table and finally to the judge.

"Mr. Hughes," said Judge Blaine, "I remind you that you are not only under oath, but an officer of the Court as well. Some serious accusations have been made about the conduct of the District Attorney, and I expect you to answer every question I put to you truthfully. Are we on the same wavelength?"

"Absolutely, your honor," though what spectrum this wavelength was in was quite beyond his grasp at the moment.

"Mr. Hughes, as an Assistant District Attorney, did you have an opportunity to speak with Martin Kilhooey around the time of a felony hearing held before Justice Lawton?"

"Yes."

"Who else was present?"

"Investigator Walter Heimlich from the Sheriff's Department."

"And do you recall what Martin Kilhooey said to you or in your presence at that time concerning the events of March 27/28, 1999?" And now Jack could see where this was going and he did not like it one little bit, and he looked at the District Attorney who was glaring at him and the jurors who looked somewhat puzzled but knew something important was happening, and he looked at his future which now was beginning to look pretty grim and he looked to his conscience and the rest was easy.

"Yes, I recall," he said with a firm voice.

"And what did he tell you?"

"He said, among other things, that he never heard Daisy Nichols return to the apartment building after 1 a.m., that when Patty Hartwick crawled out of her apartment, he had been in his bathroom and hadn't heard anything, that he didn't see Daisy Nichols until he had been out on the street, and wasn't sure whether she came from her apartment, Patty's apartment, or somewhere else."

"And did you so inform the District Attorney?"

Jack returned the angry glare from his boss with a look of sorrow. He sighed, looked at the judge, then turned to the jury and said, "I did."

The jury was excused again and both sides agreed there would be no need to call Investigator Heimlich. The District Attorney and defense counsel continued arguing the merits of the motion and the remedy sought. Finally Judge Blaine hushed them and again called the jury back.

"Ladies and gentlemen of the jury, you are probably wondering what the heck is going on here." They mostly smiled and nodded. "You have heard testimony both from the witness Martin Kilhooey and Assistant District Attorney Hughes that Martin Kilhooey once made an oral statement that was inconsistent with his testimony here in court. In fact, greatly inconsistent. It will be ultimately up to you to determine which story, if either, or any part thereof, you believe. But I am advising you of the following: the District Attorney was under a legal obligation to disclose that prior inconsistent statement to the defendant. He failed to do so. And as a result I am instructing you that you may take the District Attorney's improper conduct into consideration when determining what is the truth in this matter. In other words, you may take into consideration in weighing the proof the fact that the District Attorney of this county deliberately withheld evidence from the defendant, and from you, that might reduce the possibility that the defendant is guilty of the crime charged. That is all I will say on the subject at this time, but I intend to revisit this issue when giving you your final instructions. And now, in fairness to the defendant, I am recessing this case until tomorrow morning to give defense counsel adequate time to prepare her cross examination of the witness taking into consideration this new evidence."

The District Attorney did not dare fire Jack on the spot, but they both knew it was now only a matter of time.

Chapter 13.

Jack took his wife's hand.

"Maria, do you remember before we got married, we had a little talk and I warned you of the type of guy you were marrying? That there might come a time when we might suffer because I was too stubborn to compromise on matters of principle?"

"Oh, Jack!" she cried, looking up at him with sad, but adoring eyes. "What happened?"

So he told her everything, and in the end she really didn't understand. "Did you tell the truth?" she asked.

"Of course."

"And weren't you required to tell the truth?"

"Well, yeah."

"Then how can he fire you?"

"You don't get it, honey. I serve at the pleasure of the District Attorney. Right now, for a variety of reasons, I am most certainly not in his pleasure. There are other lawyers in this county and I have no doubt he'll find another more to his liking."

"Still," she said, "it doesn't seem fair."

And it didn't.

Remarkably, Martin Kilhooey did not wither under cross-examination the next day. In fact, he almost seemed imbued with a new confidence. He readily admitted again that he had told a different story before, but the one he told now was the same one he had told Officer Jackson up front AND the Grand Jury, and it was the TRUTH.

Surprisingly, it was Lynn Reynard who was getting flustered and frustrated. Finally, she blurted out, "Can you tell me one good reason why you would have lied to Investigator Heimlich and Assistant District Attorney Hughes?"

"Sure. 'Cause they threatened me."

BINGO. BONANZA. ACE OF ACES. ROYAL FLUSH. GRAND SLAM.

Time to sit down.

She didn't sit down.

"So, the Assistant District Attorney and an Investigator for the DeWitt County Sheriff's Department threatened you?" she asked, looking triumphantly at the District Attorney who was busy shuffling papers.

"No, not them. The Browns."

And now everybody looked up to see where this was going and, too late, Lynn Reynard sat down.

"Redirect?" asked the Judge.

"Just a few questions, your honor," said the District Attorney, smiling for the first time since the trial began.

"Mr. Kilhooey, who threatened you?"

"Objection. Irrelevant and hearsay," tried Ms. Reynard gamely.

"Overruled," said the Judge. "You opened the door and it has independent significance. Mr. Kilhooey, who threatened you?"

"Marge Brown and her son Carl and her grandson Andy and her grandson Carl."

"And what did each of them say to you?" asked the District Attorney.

"They told me if I knew what was good for me, I wouldn't say anything in..com..brinated about Daisy."

"Incriminating?"

"Yeah, that's the word they used."

"And when and where did they tell you this?"

"It was at Carl's house that Sunday night after I got back from the Sheriff's office. Marge asked me if I had signed anything and I told her no and she said I better not and she wasn't gonna let Daisy go to jail because Patty probably had it coming to her anyway, that she was bad for the family and no loss to the world. And then Carl her son says you know what can happen to people who talk too much and Andy says if you don't, my brother and I can show you and the other Carl goes yeah that's right and it won't be anything like a knife it'll be something messier so I decided to keep my mouth shut and after the Grand Jury I just told them that I lied and said I was in the crapper and didn't see anything."

"Move to strike as non-responsive," objected Ms. Reynard. "The question was when and where. Anything after that is non-responsive."

"While it may be non-responsive," ruled Judge Blaine, "only the attorney asking the question has the right to make that motion. Does the District Attorney wish the additional material stricken?"

"Not a word, your honor. And no further questions." And the District Attorney sat down.

During the suspension of Whelan Oates, Bull Heimlich had been named Acting Undersheriff, which sort of made him Acting Sheriff as well, though he wasn't pushing it too much, and the Boss was starting to make a few command decisions from his home. But Bull remembered that Whelan had been specifically ordered to do something which he had neglected to do, and now Bull reasoned that it was his duty to order himself to find out if Patty Hartwick had made any phone calls that night.

As predicted by the Sheriff, within an hour he had the answer and drove straight to the Courthouse with the information.

At the first break he handed the paper to the District Attorney, who immediately asked for a conference with the Judge with the defendant and defense counsel present.

"Judge, a new piece of evidence has just come to the attention of the People. I don't know what it means, I don't know if it is *Brady* material, but I certainly want to bring it to the attention of the Court and counsel. It is a record of phone calls made from Patty Hartwick's apartment on March 27 and March 28 of 1999."

And he handed a copy to the Judge and to Ms. Reynard, who after examining it looked puzzled and showed it to her client who betrayed nothing.

"Do you intend to interview this person ahead of time?" asked the Judge.

"I'm not sure," said the District Attorney. "In light of the other evidence, I think I'm inclined to wait until the witness is on the stand."

"And my inclination, for the moment, is the same," said Ms. Reynard.

"Well, I can't tell either one of you how to try your case, but it should be interesting," said Judge Blaine, shaking his head.

Returning to his time line, the District Attorney now commenced with meticulous detail each and every observation made by each and every police officer witness at the crime scene. Each of seventy-three photographs was carefully identified by the Sheriff's photographer Joe Probello, whose thick Italian accent slowed things down for a while. All of this took the better part of three days. It was Friday afternoon before Jack Hughes took the stand again.

Jack knew his material. His story got told in the usual straight chronology from the first call until the last goodbye when the District Attorney had no further use for him (actually, he didn't remember saying goodbye to anyone or anyone saying goodbye to him on Palm Sunday).

His description of the murder scene was detailed and graphic. He told of the blood and the mayonnaise and the strawberry jam, of the broken door knob and the broken beer bottle and the streaks on the wall, of the clothes and blood in the sink, and the bloody footprint on the kitchen floor. And then he told of Daisy Nichols and the different stories she'd been telling Bull Heimlich, and how she'd start changing details to deal with the known facts, how she claimed to have had the jars of mayonnaise and jam knocked out of her hands when Patty opened the door, and how when confronted with the stains on the door from top to bottom opined that they must have flown through the air before crashing on the door.

And Jack discussed the search waiver and how it had been unquestionably voluntary and how he had explained to Daisy her constitutional right to refuse entry.

"And did Daisy Nichols tell you whether she returned to her apartment after coming back from Marie Daley's house?"

"Yes. She consistently said that she never reentered the building because the body was in the way."

And yet, she had clearly told him that her hunting knife was in her apartment and that the door was locked with the key inside, when earlier she had said that she had left Martin Kilhooey in her apartment.

And Jack Hughes was present when that very knife was found under Daisy's mattress, still moist and with traces of blood at the hilt.

Lynn Reynard tried locking eyes with him on cross-examination, but Jack had seen Whelan Oates in the hospital bed and he didn't even need the alarm bells this time.

She tried to belittle his testimony about advising Daisy on the Constitution, adopting a haughty, mocking tone to her questions, but Jack answered in a straightforward and calm manner, never allowing himself to be twisted up by her tactics. And at last, she gave up. Jack nodded respectfully to the jury and most of them nodded back as he exited the courtroom.

And before he left the Courthouse for the weekend, and maybe for good, his boss came up to him and said, "Nice job, Jack" and it was the first compliment he had ever received from the District Attorney in the year and a half he had been working for him.

Jack Hughes spent most of the weekend catching up on work in his private office. Bull Heimlich played Sheriff, but was exceptionally flexible with the men, and called Jack twice just for the fun of it. Neil Hughes spent part of the weekend chairing a meeting of his high school class reunion committee, and convinced them that they should adopt a Moon Landing theme for the party in November. The District Attorney brought home two blank yellow legal pads and filled them. Judge Blaine played golf both Saturday and Sunday and instructed his law clerk to begin working on a charge for the jury. Whelan Oates was released from the hospital and went back to his lonely apartment and thought about calling his wife, but didn't.

And Lynn Reynard spent the weekend having difficulty forming lasting relationships.

Chapter 14.

On Monday Bull Heimlich testified, primarily about his discussions with Daisy, but also about finding the knife and his other observations of the crime scene. There followed a series of technicians linking the blood throughout the scene with the victim and establishing how useless almost every other piece of physical evidence was.

The blood on the clothes of Christy Martini and Martin Kilhooey and Daisy Nichols belonged to the decedent. The knife tested positive for blood where the blade met the hilt, but in quantities insufficient to test for type. The screwdriver used to open the door contained a number of smudged prints. The only clearly defined print was of the right index finger of Martin Kilhooey. The vague outline of a footprint in the pool of blood by the refrigerator matched in length neither the feet nor footwear of Daisy, Martin or Patty.

This latter point was repeatedly hammered home by Attorney Reynard. The District Attorney, meanwhile, emphasized that the building was not secured by the police until at least fifteen minutes after the ambulance arrived. Secretly he was more than a little peeved that the police had not gotten foot measurements from everyone who was known to have been in the vicinity, including the Brown brothers, Christy Martini, cousin Steve, all the police officers and deputies, ambulance people, etc. He didn't like hanging threads, particularly bloody ones.

The only photograph of the footprint was not particularly useful, other than a tape measure appeared in the frame. The problem was that the various witnesses who saw it with their own eyes couldn't agree on what they saw. Some thought it a bare foot, some thought it extended farther along the tape measure than others, Jack had been certain that the imprint contained a clearly defined heel of a shoe. No one else remembered that detail.

Finally, on Tuesday morning the People recalled Marjory Brown. Marge picked up her narrative with Daisy Nichols at her door. She related driving back to Fort McBain to check on the grandchildren, then the trip to the hospital. She was somewhat more vague about seeing Daisy talking to the ambulance driver, but when pressed repeated what she had told the Sheriff about Daisy admitting she had signed her name "Polly Eckler" and given a phony address because "I have my reasons." She did, however, clearly recall that Daisy at the same time was claiming to have an alibi, that she had been with Marie. This somewhat tempered the effect of the false identity as admission of wrong doing.

The narrative continued up to the return to Fort McBain and the arrival of the Sheriff. The District Attorney recalled what the Sheriff had told him about how Marge got visibly angry when she saw Daisy stroking Christy's hair to comfort her, but decided not to ask her about it.

Then, just as he looked like he was about to sit down, the District Attorney looked at Marge quizzically and said, "By the way, you had some contact with the deceased earlier that night, hadn't you?"

"Yes, I believe I testified earlier that I saw Patty in the store talking to Daisy."

"No, that's not what I mean. I'm talking about the phone call."

"What phone call?"

"The phone call you received from Patty Hartwick at approximately 11:45 p.m. on March 27, 1999," the District Attorney pressed.

"I don't know what you mean," Marge tried.

"Well, then, let me show you People's Exhibit 47 for identification and ask if that refreshes your recollection," and the District Attorney showed her the record of phone calls made from Patty Hartwick's apartment that night.

"Isn't that your phone number listed there?" and now he was in her face.

"Yes, that's my phone number, but I'm still not sure what you're getting at."

"Your honor, I request permission to treat this witness as hostile," moved the District Attorney.

"Granted," ruled the judge, thus giving him permission to lead the witness as in cross-examination.

"Isn't it true, Ms. Brown, that Patty Hartwick called you from her apartment the night she was killed and talked to you?"

A long pause. "Yes," she said weakly.

"Then tell the jury what she said to you."

"OBJECTION!" screamed Lynn Reynard, though she was not admonished for her noise level.

The jury was excused and Judge Blaine promptly commenced a hearing to determine if anything said by the defendant would be admissible under any exceptions to the hearsay rule. After the witness testified briefly about the contents of the conversation, the attorneys argued their positions. The only pertinent exceptions were if it were a dying declaration or an excited utterance, as those terms had been defined by prior case law. The District Attorney argued that they were both.

"If, as the witness stated, the first words out of Patty's mouth were 'Daisy stabbed me', she might very well have been under the belief that she was dying, even though we know now that the fatal wound did not come until later. And even if it wasn't a dying declaration, it certainly qualifies as an excited utterance coming as it does immediately after the event she was relating."

"And that," said Ms. Reynard, "is precisely the problem with the People's argument. We don't KNOW precisely when the alleged stabbing took place. The only witness with a time line was Martin Kilhooey and even if he is to be believed, he was less than certain of the time and an excited utterance can not be anything other than contemporaneous with the event. Case law is very clear on that. And as for dying declaration, we can not throw away the hearsay rule simply on speculation. There is NO evidence before the Court as to whether Patty thought she was dying when the statement was made, only the musings of the District Attorney."

The District Attorney took another shot. "The purposes of the exceptions to the hearsay rule carved out by the courts were to ensure the reliability of out of court statements used to establish the truth. The statement 'Daisy stabbed me', made when we know from the admission of the defendant herself to Marie Daley that Patty was covered with blood, taken with the totality of the evidence in *this case*, not any other case, points to this statement of the deceased being reliable, and in any event sufficiently reliable for the jury to consider it with all of the other evidence. They can make that determination as well as you can."

"The Court should not piggy-back a hearsay statement into this case," argued Ms. Reynard and remained standing with a pleading look in her eye that the judge, who was always watching her, could plainly see. And he liked what he saw.

"The Court finds that there is no exception to the hearsay rule which would permit the introduction of this testimony. The objection is sustained, and I will advise the jury that they are not to speculate on the contents of the telephone conversation." And that was that.

When the jury returned and had been duly admonished, the District Attorney asked the witness, "Did you have any further contact with the deceased that evening other than what you have already testified to?"

"No."

On cross-examination, Ms. Reynard, recalling what Whelan had told her about what the Sheriff had told him about how Marge got visibly angry when she saw Daisy stroking Christy's hair to comfort her, decided not to ask her about it.

Feeling lucky, she asked a final question. "You never threatened Martin Kilhooey in any way to make him change his testimony in this case, did you?"

"Certainly not," Marge replied.

And on that feeble note, the People rested.

Lynn Reynard had two hours before court resumed to prepare her defense, engaging in intense conversations with her client.

"Do you wish to present any evidence on behalf of the defendant?" inquired Judge Blaine.

"No, your honor, the Defendant, Daisy Nichols, rests," said Lynn Reynard, mustering as much confidence in her voice as she could.

As soon as the Judge set closing arguments for the next morning, the lone reporter scurried out of the courtroom to file her story, the District Attorney shook his head in disbelief, the court reporter packed up her gear, and the judge smiled at Lynn Reynard and she smiled back.

"You each made a promise to me," began Ms. Reynard in summation to the jury. "You each told me that Daisy Nichols sits here innocent until the government has proved the case against her *beyond* a **REASONABLE DOUBT**. Now, after hearing the government's case, it is more important than ever that you keep that promise, because the evidence presented here should reasonably cause you to have more questions than answers, and if you have questions, you have doubts, and if you have doubts in this case, you have reasonable doubts, and if you have reasonable doubts, then Daisy Nichols is innocent in the eyes of the law and you **CAN NOT** find her guilty.

"Now, let's be frank. I suspect some of you are already thinking that she might have done it, or even that she probably did it, and are worried, genuinely worried, that if you find her not guilty, that somehow, some way she might be getting away with something and you don't want to see that happen. Well, ladies and gentlemen, if you start thinking that way, and start acting on those thoughts, then you are already violating the oaths you took and the solemn promises you made to my client.

"This Presumption of Innocence doctrine didn't just spring up overnight. It is an ancient and honored tradition in Anglo-Saxon jurisprudence," continued Ms. Reynard, enrapturing her mostly Anglo-Saxon jury. "It is one of the basic liberties of the people, a protection of the weak from the powerful. It used to be that people could be thrown in jail for a long time on the whim of a government official. Well, we don't do that any more, but the price of this freedom did not come cheap, and even the soil of this valley is stained with the blood of those who would die rather than give up these rights to be protected from the powerful force of the government. That's why we have courts, that's why we have constitutions, that's why we have juries: to protect the weak and level the playing field and make us all equal under the law.

"Someone once said that the Presumption of Innocence is the Golden Thread of our Law, and it has been said many times that it is better for ten guilty people to go free than that one innocent person should be convicted, for to do so is to spit in the face of justice!" She got that one from watching *Rumpole*.

They were listening. And so, she began reviewing the testimony with them, suggesting alternate explanations and theories, reminding them that they need not adopt any of these theories, but merely have doubts, which were *certainly* reasonable under the circumstances.

"Ultimately the government's case against Daisy Nichols hangs on the testimony of one man, Martin Kilhooey, a man who by the testimony of everyone who knows him is not to be trusted in matters of TRUTH, a man who was fully capable of having committed the crimes himself, a man who owned the screwdriver used to pry open the door to Patty Hartwick's apartment, whose fingerprint was the only one found on that screwdriver, a man who remained behind while Daisy spent critical time at the home of Marie Daley, a man found lurking in an alley next to the apartments when the neighbors were coming to help. Why should you believe ONE WORD of his testimony?

"And even if you do believe him, which is nearly impossible, the evidence fairly shows that he was *at least* an accomplice, a man involved in the unlawful entry of Patty Hartwick's apartment for the purpose of committing a crime therein, and the judge will instruct you that if you find he is an accomplice *as a **Matter of Law*** you cannot credit ONE WORD of his testimony unless you find his testimony is independently corroborated. And I ask you, *where is that corroboration?* Certainly not in the evidence presented by the government.

"This same government that tried to keep you from learning that Martin Kilhooey had previously told them a completely different story, this same government that can't find a foot to match the footprint in the blood in Patty Hartwick's kitchen, this same government that intimidates a young woman into agreeing to give up her constitutional right to be secure in her own home, and then breaks into her apartment to protect the people of Fort McBain from a *stove that was too hot*, or some *chicken that was too raw*," she said dripping with sarcasm, "this same government wants you to believe that Daisy Nichols brutally attacked and killed Patty Hartwick because . . .well, because why? Because she quit her job? Because she made too much noise? Because she . . .*didn't want her mayonnaise back?* Ladies and gentlemen, does any of that make any sense to you *whatsoever*?

"You know my client didn't testify, and you know she doesn't have to, and you know you all promised me that if she didn't testify you wouldn't hold it against her, and you know that you *can't* hold it against her without violating the solemn oaths you took. At the end of the government's case we rested and as a result we proved nothing to you, not only because under the law we *have* nothing to prove to you, but because that is precisely what the government proved against Daisy Nichols: *absolutely nothing.*

"Under our procedure, this is the last time I am allowed to address you, and the government's representative, the District Attorney, gets to have the last word before the Judge gives you his final instructions. I hope I haven't done anything in this courtroom to annoy you or aggravate you or cause you any sort of discomfort. But if I have, please don't take it out on Daisy Nichols. It is not her fault that she was assigned a young and inexperienced attorney to represent her against the power of the state. I hope what I have said makes some sense to you, but if it hasn't, use your own powers of thought and your own wisdom and your own respect for human liberty to reach the right conclusion, the only reasonable conclusion, a verdict of *not guilty.*"

She paused. She scanned them individually with professional eyes. She thanked them. She sat down.

The District Attorney rose. "Ladies and gentlemen, you just heard some very pretty words from the attorney for the defendant, and I must admit that she does very pretty very well."

"Objection," said the very pretty Ms. Reynard.

"Counsel approach," sighed Judge Blaine.

At the side bar, Judge Blaine inquired, "Surely you are not suggesting that the District Attorney spoke untruthfully?"

She smiled. "Certainly not, your honor, but it is no more appropriate for the District Attorney to comment on my looks than it would be for me to comment on his buns."

The District Attorney unconsciously reached to cover his behind, then caught himself.

"I apologize, your honor. I certainly meant no offense."

"Do you want a corrective instruction?" asked the judge.

"No, your honor, the apology is sufficient," she said.

"Good. Then let's continue."

As the attorneys turned to head back to their previous positions, Lynn Reynard whispered, "Nice buns" and the District Attorney blushed but raised no objection.

"As I was saying," the District Attorney recommenced, "those are pretty words, and many of them important words, but I fail to see their connection to this case. The attorney for the defendant kept saying 'the government, the government, the government' over and over as if this were Nazi Germany or Stalinist Russia or the Spanish Inquisition. The last I checked *I* wasn't an agent of George III or Bad Prince John. I'm just a guy elected to be the District Attorney by the good people of this county, just like the Sheriff who ran this investigation was elected by the same people, and the judge here. None of us gets paid any more if you convict the defendant or if you let her go. We've all got a job to do and so do you. I hope I've done a good job and the best I know how, and I hope the same for the sheriff and the judge and even Ms. Reynard here.

"I do not represent **The Government**. I represent the **People** and that is why this indictment was brought in the name of the **People of the State of New York**, the same **People** who, in legislature assembled, determined through their lawful and freely elected representatives, that it should be a crime for one person to take the life of another.

"And that is why we are here: to see that the person who took the life of Patty Hartwick is brought to justice."

Then began a methodical, point by point by point, recapitulation of the evidence in the case, a presentation that lasted for the next two and a half hours. Evidence bags were opened, items displayed, reports reviewed, and finally People's Exhibit One.

"Ms. Reynard says Martin Kilhooey was an accomplice, ladies and gentlemen, and that his story needs corroboration. Well, here it is!" and he held the knife aloft.

"You have been reminded that the defendant didn't have to testify in this case, and that is true, and the judge will instruct you that you are to draw absolutely no inference from her failure to testify, and that is as it should be. BUT, you have heard from the defendant, in the words she spoke to Marie Daley, to Investigator Heimlich, to Assistant District Attorney Hughes, to the other witnesses in this case, and you may certainly consider those, even if you find they may not have been completely truthful.

"Ladies and gentlemen, the defendant told Investigator Heimlich that she never went back into her apartment after returning from Marie Daley's house and finding the body of Patty Hartwick blocking the front door. We know from Marie Daley that there is absolutely no question that the defendant carried this very knife with her when she left the Daley house. So, ladies and gentlemen, I ask you . . .*how did this knife, a knife with traces of blood at the hilt, a knife still moist when found by investigator Heimlich, how did this knife suddenly appear between the mattress and the box spring of Daisy Nichol's bed, in Daisy Nichols' apartment, behind Daisy Nichols' locked door, a door that Daisy Nichols said she knew was locked?"*

He continued to hold the knife steady while letting this sink in, then continued quietly.

"There is your corroboration, ladies and gentlemen. Only the defendant could have put that knife there. Only the defendant would have had a reason to hide that knife. Only the defendant could have viciously and heinously stabbed Patty Hartwick and then left her to bleed to death while she tried to cover up her crime. There is no *reasonable* doubt here, ladies and gentlemen. There is no doubt here at all. The right person was arrested, and on the case presented the right person will be convicted, that is. . . . if you all do what you must, and that is to weigh all the evidence, use your common sense and judgment, and return a verdict of GUILTY."

After lunch the judge gave his final instructions to the jury. That charge to the jury included general instructions on principles of law, and specific instructions relating to the facts of the case. He reminded the jury again, that based on the misconduct of the District Attorney they were free to take the most negative inference possible with respect to the credibility of the testimony of Martin Kilhooey. He gave a long and elaborate and, in the mind of the District Attorney, "pro-defense" charge on the use of circumstantial evidence.

He told them that, on the evidence, they could find that Martin Kilhooey was an accomplice in the crimes, and must make that determination before proceeding further.

"The law says that a defendant may not be convicted of any offense upon the testimony of an accomplice unsupported by corroborative evidence tending to connect the defendant with the commission of such offense. Under that law Miss Nichols may not be convicted solely on the testimony of a witness who is an accomplice. Our law views with suspicion the testimony of an accomplice in a criminal trial, since he was a participant in the events charged in the indictment.

"If you find there is no such corroborative evidence, you MUST disregard entirely the testimony of the accomplice, Martin Kilhooey, and strike his testimony from your minds.

"On the other hand, if you find such other evidence sufficient, then you may consider the testimony of Martin Kilhooey, consistent with the admonishment I have previously given you with respect to the misconduct of the District Attorney, together with all the other evidence in the case, in making your final determination of the guilt or innocence of Daisy Nichols."

An hour and fifteen minutes later, at 4:42 P.M., Judge Samuel R. Blaine concluded his instructions to the jury and deliberation, at last, began.

In chambers, robe off and settling back in his exceptionally comfortable judicial high-back leather chair, Judge Blaine asked the attorneys, "Any possibility of settling this now that the proof is in?"

"All or nothing, your honor," said the District Attorney, so the defense counsel had no reason to consider the possibility.

The judge put his hands behind his head, kicked his feet up, and addressed Lynn Reynard. "Regardless of the outcome, you did a hell of a job for your client, counselor. I've got to say, it takes maturity and nerves of steel to keep your client off the stand."

"That and her client's prior perjury conviction," chimed in the District Attorney who stopped chuckling when he noticed the judge's icy glare.

"Well, I thank you for the compliment and all your consideration during the trial," said Lynn, as sincerely as she was capable of being. "I must say I was very impressed with your handling of the trial and your grasp of the law," she added.

"Well," said the judge, "maybe before we start singing 'Mutual Admiration Society' we should take a break. The jury will be in there for a while. Go get something to eat. Just let the court officer know where you'll be in case you're needed."

The jury decided to have food brought in and worked through dinner. At 7:45 p.m. everyone returned to the courtroom with a question from the jury.

"Your honor," said the foreman, "what some of us want to know is, if we find that Martin Kilhooey is an accomplice *and* there is no other collaborating evidence, do we *have* to find the defendant not guilty of murder, *even if we believe every word of his testimony?*"

"First of all," said the judge, "the word is 'corroborating' evidence, and yes, what you say is correct, or rather, to put it another way, if you find he is an uncorroborated accomplice, you may not even *consider* his testimony."

The jury was excused to continue deliberations.

The question had frozen the two attorneys.

"*Now* do you want to discuss settlement?" asked the judge.

My God, they're thinking about throwing out the only direct evidence connecting her with the murder, worried the District Attorney. *On the other hand, they talked about believing every word of Martin Kilhooey. If they really believe him, they'll never find he was an accomplice, or if they do, they'll find some corroboration. On the other hand, they might just follow the judge's instructions to the letter. Nahhh. They'd never let her off if they think she did it. Or would they?*

At the next table, Ms. Reynard similarly mused. *They bought into the accomplice stuff, Martin isn't credible anyway, the judge already basically told them to ignore his testimony. What we're looking at here is at most an assault second on the slugging incident. Say, is Judge Blaine undressing me with his eyes? That rascal.*

She spoke briefly with her client. "The defendant does not wish to consider any settlement offers at this time, your honor," said attorney Reynard, so the District Attorney had no reason to consider the possibility.

By Friday evening the jury had still not reached a verdict and they were sequestered for the weekend.

Chapter 15.

On that spectacular October Sunday, with the air as crisp as the first bite of a MacIntosh apple, as Charles Kuralt once said, John Robert Hughes, Jr. became a Christian and the newest member of St. Mary's parish. On his behalf his Godparents, big cousins Anna and Neil, Jr., duly rejected Satan and all his works and all his empty promises and meanwhile nobody connected in any way with the baptism was getting shot at or otherwise assassinated, though doubtless the Prince of Darkness and Father of Lies was being kept busy somewhere in the universe. *Just not here, in this holy place, among these wonderful people*, thought Jack as he put one arm around his wonderful wife and used the other to balance wonderful little Laura somewhat precariously on his hip in the soft candlelight of the church as they all gathered round the baptismal font.

The elderly priest performed the ritual and blessed the parents and the child and threw in a blessing for Laura as well, who was already beaming with pride over "her baby". Afterwards he said, "You know, Jack, it doesn't seem like so long ago we were pouring water over *your* little head. I remember I put the salt on your lips and you started slurping it up like you hadn't eaten in a week!" They all laughed.

"But you know, it really is a wonderful feeling to have lived long enough to see the results of God's handiwork in you and Maria and Laura and now Little Jack. I remember your parents, God rest them, and your grandparents even. How long has it been for your father now?"

"Twenty-five years in December," said Jack after a moment.

"That long. Yes, you were so young. A good man. A very good man. He was on our first Parish Council, you know." Jack nodded. "And your mother. Well, I don't have to tell you about your mother. If we don't unveil a statue of her in here some day,. . . well, then, we ought to.

"Welcome to God's People, Little Jack," he said in final farewell, and disappeared into the sacristy, wiping something from his eye.

At the party afterwards in the old family homestead that Jack and Maria had bought from his mother's estate, Jack made a big hit with his lasagna, cooked with the same Italian sauce that Mom used to make, layered in the same careful way with the same ingredients, and devoured in the same old fashioned way by her children, in-laws and grandchildren. Maria surprised everyone, including Jack, with a Holiday Pie *a la Mom*, with the wonderfully familiar flaky crust and the puddings and cream and puddings-and-cream that had always made it such a big hit. *Mom is here,* thought Jack, and knew it was true.

After dinner the adults and older kids raised their wine glasses while Neil gave the toast.

"*A la familia!*" he said, and that was all he needed to say.

During halftime of the second football game, Neil and Jack sat in the old kitchen.

"What do you think, Neil. Is there really a devil? I mean, somebody named Satan or Lucifer or Beelzebub or Scratch or whatever, who consciously wanders the world seeking the ruination of souls?"

Neil smiled. "I don't know for sure, Jack, but I've seen no empirical evidence to the contrary and more than a little to support the theory.

"I don't know whether Evil has a name or a consciousness or a specific agenda. But there is evil in the world, Jack, and you never know where it's going to land and you'd better hope and pray that it doesn't land on you, or that if it does land on you that you have the courage and the strength to fight it off. Some people just give up fighting. I think we all know some of them."

Jack thought about that. "It seems to land on some people more than others, I think."

"Nobody's immune, Jack. Nobody. And if you do get into a battle with him, if it *is* a him, well, sometimes he'll just walk away. Other times, it just seems to whet his appetite and he starts smelling the big prize and comes after you twice as hard. There's no telling. Just got to be ready for him, any time . . . all the time."

For a while, they said nothing.

"May it never land on us, or anyone dear to us," said Jack solemnly as they raised their Harps.

"Deliver us from evil," intoned Neil in reply and they returned to the game.

Whelan tried, but he just couldn't get her out of his head. Night and day the thought of her tormented him. He kept reliving every moment, the wonderful stuff, the bad stuff, the joy, the ecstacy, the rage, the loneliness, the emptiness. Mostly the emptiness: that deep, hollow, numb, worthless, agonized feeling, the deadened silence and the cacophony of demons. There were times when he felt this surge in his brain, could actually feel and distinguish the different chemicals reaching out and stimulating the nerve paths so that in a split second he felt, distinctly, the entire range of human emotions. Sometimes it almost felt like a ping-pong game, with that little depression ball bouncing cheerfully from one side of his head to the other, and always, always, she was there, sometimes smiling, sometimes gazing lovingly, sometimes staring at him with quivering jaw and abject contempt, and sometimes just . . . ignoring him.

Every once in a while a memory of his wife and his child tried to push its way to the fore, but the demons quickly crushed it and silenced it. He knew she must be thinking of him too, had to be. Even if it was over, they had shared so much, given so much of themselves to each other emotionally, and physically, that surely, surely part of him was still with her and haunting her in the same way he was now haunted.

He could not have known, would not have suspected, that Lynn Reynard thought of him not at all, not a bit, not an iota. From endless practice she had been able to complete cleanse herself of each experience of love and move on. Nothing learned, nothing gained, nothing lost, nothing left. *Never have I once looked back to sigh over a romance behind me* she might have sung if she were playing the lead in *Oklahoma!*, but chances were she wouldn't have even thought about it *that* much. She lived her life in the perpetual joy of new love, and when, as it must, love began to wither and decay and use an enforced ceremony, it was an easy thing for her to merely fall in love all over again and leave it for others to clean up the destruction.

Night after night the demons drove Whelan on, until he found himself, often, parked in his car down the street from her apartment where he could watch her come and go from a discrete distance, and watch others come and go, and sometimes stay.

The tears didn't flow anymore, although sometimes he wished they would, wished for release. But there was no release, and there were no tears. Nothing but pain, and numbness, and deadening silence, and emptiness and that merry little ping-pong ball.

On Monday morning once again the jury assembled and once again were remanded to the sanctity of the jury room to recommence deliberations.

This time, in under two hours, they passed a note to the judge indicating a verdict had been reached.

And now the nonchalance of the preceding days ended and a sudden bustle of activity broke out in the courthouse. Attorneys and the press were summoned, employees from around the building gathered in the visitors' gallery, as did the few relatives of Daisy Nichols, and Daisy herself took her place by her attorney, and the District Attorney unconsciously buttoned his jacket and straightened his tie and the clerk took her place and the court reporter limbered her fingers and the court officer pounded thrice on the wooden door and shouted ALL RISE IN HONOR OF THE COURT and Judge Samuel R. Blaine solemnly entered and took his place behind the elaborately carved mahogany bench.

And now all remained standing for the jury, in honor of their noble authority and the Common Law and the Magna Carta and the Constitutions of the United States and the State of New York and the Bill of Rights and the Inalienable Rights and Justice and Truth.

When all were seated, Judge Blaine asked the foreman to stand.

"Has the jury reached a verdict?" asked the judge.

"We have," said the foreman.

"And is that verdict unanimous?"

"It is."

And then the judge turned the whole matter over to the Clerk of the Court while the defendant stood and faced the jury with her attorney.

"On the first count of the indictment, Murder in the Second Degree," intoned the Clerk, "how do you find?"

Days come and days go, hours fly and time passes and it is most rare that we give a *particular* moment any consideration whatsoever. But, comes a time when a lifetime is in the balance and then, ah, then heartbeats stop and breath is caught and all nature freezes in place and eternity groans and *what next* seems nigh unto forever and that moment burns, burns into the psyche until finally in one great gush it is over.

"We find the defendant Guilty," said the foreman, calmly.

And so on for each of the other counts, guilty as charged.

Daisy Nichols betrayed little emotion. Her attorney quivered a bit, but for once no eyes were on her and no one noticed.

"Does the defendant wish the jury to be polled?" asked Judge Blaine.

"We do, your honor," said Ms. Reynard.

One by one, on each of the charges, the individual members of the jury were polled and each time each one said "Guilty" and none looked at the defendant.

Finally, the jury was discharged with the thanks of the Court and after exchanging pleasantries with the judge and the attorneys they went back to their lives.

When order was restored and the jury departed, Attorney Reynard made a perfunctory motion for a dismissal of the charges notwithstanding the verdict.

Before the District Attorney could reply, Judge Blaine ruled, "All post trial motions are reserved for the time of sentencing, which will be scheduled for December 3, 1999 at 9:30 a.m. The defendant is remanded to the custody of the sheriff without bail pending sentence or further order of this Court."

And it was over.

Jack Hughes was handling the end of the morning calendar in Sanford Mills City Court when the District Attorney entered the Courtroom.

"Your honor, may I have a moment with the Assistant District Attorney?"

"Of course," said the kindly City Court Judge.

This is it, thought Jack. The end.

"Jack, I just want you to know the jury returned guilty verdicts on all counts."

"Congratulations, boss," said Jack sincerely.

"I think there's something we need to talk about. I think you know what it is."

"I'm listening," said Jack, deciding there was no reason he should make this any easier for the District Attorney.

"About your testimony. I talked to a couple of the jurors. They told me that your testimony made all the difference in the case. With all the screws-loose and screw-ups and screwballs they decided they could believe you completely. And you know why, Jack?"

All Jack could do was shake his head.

"Because they said that anybody who wouldn't lie to save his own job must be telling the truth. See you tomorrow."

And with that, he left.

Lynn Reynard sat facing Judge Blaine in chambers.

"I know how it feels," he said. "Lost a few in my time. But you can't keep second guessing yourself. Just move on to the next one. You think you can do that?"

"I'm sure of it," said the attorney.

The judge's secretary intruded. "Just want to remind you, Judge, that you have a class reunion coming up. This is your third notice. What should I tell them?"

"Just leave it here. I'll take care of it," he said and dismissed her.

"I never go to those things," he explained to Lynn. "Everybody showing off pictures of their kids and reliving old glories. Frankly, high school was not that happy a time for me. Besides, I've got nobody to go with, so I don't need LOSER added to my other high school laurels."

"Now, Judge," said Lynn Reynard carefully, "It seems to me you could be telling me this for one of two reasons. Either you are looking for a little sympathy, or you could be signaling that you'd be interested in taking me."

Judge Blaine started, then looked at her a moment before replying, "Maybe it's a little bit of both. But, of course, it probably wouldn't be proper with you still having this case in front of me. The reunion is Thanksgiving weekend and the sentencing is after that."

"Is it out of town?"

"Way out of town."

"Well, then, I doubt very much there would be anybody there who would know anything about me or this case, and if nobody knows about it, who cares? It's not like I'm trying to actually influence you."

"So," he asked as casually as he could, "do you want to go with me?"

"I'd be delighted. I think we'd have a lot of fun."

"Well, then," he smiled. "I guess it's a date, then."

"It's a date," she said entrancingly.

Chapter 16.

In many places across the Northeast the traditional date for high school class reunions is the Saturday after Thanksgiving, and so on November 27, 1999 Mike and Genevieve Sullivan tentatively stepped through the door of Gold Harbor's biggest banquet hall.

They need not have worried. They were immediately surrounded by the friendly faces of Faith's classmates, pleased beyond words that their invitation had finally been accepted. They were quickly swept up to a place of honor where all night long they caught up on the lives of the not-so-young-anymore graduates of the Bishop McClure High School Class of 1969.

They had thought it would be hard, but the memories tonight were all pleasant ones, wonderful old stories of high school adventures and pranks and hijinx. They learned that their daughter had a mischievous side to her, and hearing these tales for the first time was like uncovering a hidden treasure in your attic and nearly brought her back to life.

A table had been set for the departed, service for six now, so that all would be present in spirit. During the course of the evening nearly everyone stopped by that table and paused and reflected. The Sullivans kissed their daughter's picture, and remembered the others as well: the young mother with the brain tumor, the lad with the congenital heart defect who died the same summer as Faith, the former Peace Corps volunteer dead at 40 from Lou Gehrig's disease, the fellow crushed by snow from the roof of his woodshed, the girl killed in an auto accident a week after graduating from college, the business executive with the sudden heart attack. All gone, every one just as dead as Faith.

After dinner a local DJ played dance music, specializing in hits of the sixties, an era never quite understood by the Sullivans, though they were tolerant. Still, Genevieve managed to tune it out and in her mind's eye she drifted back to the late 1940's and her sailor home from the war and the big bands and the cotillion balls and the fancy dresses and her hair all done up and that big, strong handsome Mike Sullivan sweeping her across the dance floor and dreaming away into the night with the world at peace and their whole big, bright wonderful future ahead of them.

The class president walked up to the DJ and whispered in his ear, and before long the sixties songs were set aside and out came the old songs, the good songs, the songs with melody and heart and joy and poignancy and memories. And Big Mike, older and grayer and stiffer, looked through his fading eyes and saw his high school sweetheart, the one who had waited for him through that long awful conflict, the one who that warm summer day had become his bride, the one who had been by his side through every joy and sorrow and tragedy for over fifty years, and he grabbed her and swept her off her feet again and a big hole opened for them on the dance floor and for those precious moments all was as it had been, and as it always should be.

~

For the first time since the baby was born, Jack and Maria hired a babysitter and partied away. It was fifteen years for Jack and his classmates at St. Mary's High School, a somewhat less traditional year for a reunion, so the attendance was down a bit from their tenth, but theirs had been a partying class, and, as a charter member of SGT (Seniors for Good Times), Jack would not have missed it for anything.

Unlike most spouses at class reunions, Maria actually enjoyed Jack's. She had only been a year behind him in school, so she knew most everybody and several of her own friends had married Jack's classmates so it was as much a reunion for them as it was for the others.

"Maria! I hear you had another baby!" and that was all it took for the moms group to start comparing notes and strategies.

"My pediatrician recommends a glass of beer once a day while nursing. Says the liquid helps the milk flow, the alcohol relaxes the mother and puts her in a better mood for dealing with the baby and the residual alcohol in the breast milk has a calming effect on the child."

As scientifically interesting as this was, Jack felt it was more than he needed to know at the moment and excused himself from his wife and started mixing with the old gang.

"So, Jack, how are things in the District Attorney's office?"

"Well, I was recently involved in a murder investigation."

"Same old, same old, eh? You know Jack, with two kids now you really should be thinking about life insurance."

"Actually I have a $100,000 policy at work."

"Don't plan on staying dead long do you? Now I can set you up with this plan . . ."

Across town Neil and Mary Hughes stepped into outer space.

Aluminum foil stars with the names of their classmates hung from the ceiling, an ice sculpture of a lunar lander graced the center of the room, and the back wall was covered with a giant mural of the surface of the moon with an American flag sticking out of it. Across the front of the head table was a banner reading, "We came in peace for all mankind." Neil, who had designed the whole thing, was mighty proud.

"Neil, I'm surprised you didn't put green cheese on the tables," giggled Gail Wells.

"Now, Gail, as you know, technically the moon is not composed of green cheese," interrupted Tom Budoniak, MIT grad. "The surface is composed of a combination of volcanic ash and . . ."

"That's ok, Tommy, I'll read the book," she said as she giggled off to another table.

Neil turned around and nearly knocked over a tall, lean former basketball player.

"Neil Hughes, I hope," he said, feigning wit.

"Jimbo! Is that you? How's the writing trade? I hear you left me out of your last three books," said Neil, a trifle jealously.

"Gotta be careful when you write about lawyers. Don't need to get myself sued. What do you think, Mary, should I put some of those old stories about Neil in my next book?"

"Jim, there is no way that his career could survive your treatment, no matter how much gloss you put on his sordid past! Please, for the sake of our children . . ."

"Not to worry, Mary. I'll keep him out of it as a favor to you. Although that thing between him and Gail Wells in eighth grade is kinda hard to resist!"

"Jim. . ."

"OK, OK. Tell you what, Neil. We'll make a deal. You don't write about me and I won't write about you. Whadya say?"

"Deal," said Neil, with his lawyer fingers crossed behind his back.

Just then the class president, a retired US Air Force colonel, took the microphone.

"Ladies and gentlemen, fellow classmates, I hope I haven't overstepped my authority here, but in keeping with the spirit of the occasion I've decided to invite a friend of mine to be our special guest tonight. Let's have a nice warm Sanford Mills welcome for. . . Buzz Aldrin!"

"Mary," said Neil, "I can see that this is gonna be my kinda night!"

~

"Sammy Blaine! Still looking for a date for the junior prom?" teased Pete Menoir.

What a thigh-slapper. No wonder we called him Pete Manure.

"Pete! How nice to see you! Let me introduce my friend Lynn Reynard."

Pete was impressed. Very impressed. Shocked in fact.

"How nice to meet you, Mr. . .?"

"Menoir. Rhymes with Renoir, you know, the painter?"

"Well, then you must be good at first impressions," she retorted and they all laughed gaily though Pete didn't really get it.

She took the Judge's arm as they went around the room, eventually letting her hand slip into his. The occasional squeeze made him all the more certain that this had been a marvelous idea. A number of members of his Rogues Gallery were present, and he made sure he introduced each of those withered, sallow crones to this vibrant, radiant, spectacularly gorgeous young thing who made him feel like he was the only man in the world.

If she was playing a part, she was playing it to the hilt. She was charming, beautiful, delightful, witty, intoxicating. And when she looked at him she looked straight into his eyes and locked on lovingly with just a *hint* of longingly. And everyone could see it. For this night, she was . . . PERFECT.

He nearly giggled at the thought of the rest of them and how they must feel now. Here he was, not only successful but with the trophy babe on his arm. He knew there would be whispers off in the corners again, like before, only now he was not the object of scorn or ridicule or pity. He was . . .TRIUMPHANT. *Genesis 1:28*, he addressed them all silently, individually and collectively. She was better than all of them, except maybe for that one who wasn't here, the other one with those green eyes and the soft blond hair, the smile, the laugh. No, better than her. Much better.

It was getting late and the DJ was slowing down, so he pulled out an old Sinatra tune, a chestnut even way back in 1969, and long before that even. Sam touched her hand and led her gently to the dance floor. He knew all eyes were on them. And he LOVED IT!

> *It seems we stood and talked like this before*
> *We looked at each other in the same way then,*
> *But I can't remember where or when.*

Her face was next to his. She let go of his hand and flung her arms around his neck. If they were any closer they would have been behind each other. They glided.

The clothes you're wearing are the clothes you wore.
The smile you are smiling you were smiling then,
But I can't remember where or when.

The blue-eyed one crooned on.

He looked at her, in a trance. "Is it real?" he asked.

Her eyes answered first, then she did. "This is as real as it gets."

She buried her face in his chest to wipe away that small tear of happiness.

Yes, he thought. *This is the way it was always supposed to be. Yes. Oh, yes!*

Some things that happened for the first time,
Seem to be happening again.

"I don't know about you, " she whispered in his ear, " but I feel like we're two teenagers in love forever."

Yes. Just like it should have been that other time, with that other one, the one with the green eyes and the soft blond hair and that confidant look and that majestic something and that smile that should have been only for him. The one who wasn't here.

He swept her around the floor and they melted into a dream..

And so it seems that we have met before,
And laughed before,
And loved before,
But who knows where or when?

Chapter 17.

They were staying at the old Blaine homestead. Sam's mother had flown to California to spend the holiday with her sister, never thinking that Sam might come home. He simply never had before. She had been a bit upset about missing him, but he promised they would get together soon.

Sam had put Lynn in his old room while he gallantly took what had always been the guest bedroom, at least since his grandmother had died in 1957. It's not that the thought of consummating this new relationship hadn't occurred to them. Indeed, when they had finally been alone after the reunion they had lost no time in exploring each other deeply and passionately. But Lynn had a rule about not sleeping with a fellow until the sixth date, at least the ones she considered potentially serious long-term investments, and Sam was not about to jeopardize his first love in years by moving too quickly. Besides, there was always the possibility of that old Bob Dole Syndrome surfacing again, and that could certainly put the kibosh on the relationship quickly. *Take it slow. Nice and easy. There's always tomorrow.*

Sam's room was pretty much as he had left it thirty years earlier. There were a few scholastic achievement certificates on one wall and a poster of Bob Dylan on another. The bed was a twin size with a simple maple headboard and foot board and a matching four-drawer dresser and mirror next to it. A student desk and chair stood in a corner. Sam's high school senior picture sat on top of the desk, no doubt a later addition by his mother. Everything was neater than it should be, but then there had been no one to mess it up in quite a while. Sam had never stayed here for more than a couple of days since he left for college in the late summer of 1969

Lynn Reynard was the curious sort, and before retiring she opened all the drawers in the room and checked the closet. The latter was used for seasonal storage by Mrs. Blaine. The dresser was completely empty. The desk contained old high school papers and notebooks of Sam's.

In the top desk drawer she found a blue spiral notebook with the handwritten title, "Rogues Gallery" on the front. *I've heard of this. Didn't Sam use that phrase earlier in the evening? I don't think he ever explained it.*

She opened it up and flipped through at random. *Poetry. I hate poetry.* But it was a different kind of poetry. Teenage poetry, definitely, but of an archaic type. *This isn't the kind of stuff anyone wrote when I was a teenager.* It was. . .what? Shakespearean? She tried hard to think and remember something about that, but it was no use. That stuff had never been retained, pushed out by more important things.

She read a few and found them rather funny. Sam had a way of deftly putting people down. She admired that, wished her own wit was a little sharper. Still, it was all that puppy love stuff. She saw some signs of that Junior Prom date that Pete Manure had talked about earlier. *No, wait, that wasn't his real name. What was it? Manet? Monet? Hell, they all blend in together. Menoir, that was it. First impressions.* And she laughed again at her own joke and thought herself rather a wit after all.

She flipped through a few more and noticed a darker mood in some of the later ones, including number "XII":

> *She came and went. I hardly felt her go.*
> *And once again the thoughts of time left dead —*
> *And now the sleep arrives, that ebb and flow*
> *That comforts not as sleep of night. Instead*
> *I wander dim through life and fight despair,*
> *Try hard to still the beat of ravens' wings,*
> *A swooning sickness worse than* mal de mer,
> *Rushing through the thistles, scorpion stings.*
> *My mouth is dry and clotted thick with sand.*
> *The eyes begin to bulge, I gasp for breath.*
> *I pray for hope ---- deliverance at hand ---*
> *Alive and living sordid, soulless death.*
> *I must arise and face it as it comes -----*
> *But pain becomes a habit ---- and soon numbs.*

Yucckk!!
The door opened.
"Where'd you find that?" asked Judge Blaine.
"Oh, it was lying around. You really had quite a way with words. I never dreamed you were a secret poet!"
"Old garbage," he replied and took the notebook from her and sat next to her on the bed.
"I just came in to say goodnight and pleasant dreams."
"Well, thank you for a lovely evening and pleasant dreams to you, too. And one more thing. I think it would be so very nice if you wrote a poem for me."

He laughed. "It's been a while. On the other hand, you are the source of much inspiration. I've been actually thinking of a couple for you, but they're still percolating. Give me a few days."

"Well, just one more thing, and then I'll let you go. I haven't decided what I should call you."

How about "Judge"?

"Call me whatever you like. . . Just call me!" he said instead and was immediately sorry because now she'd be comparing him to Martin Kilhooey in her head and that was no way to get to first base.

"I was thinking of 'Sam' or 'Sammy', but then I heard that impressionist call you 'Sammy' and I didn't like it. I think 'Samuel'. What do you think?"

"Fine by me, Miss Reynard."

"Lynn."

"Goodnight, Lynn" and his lips covered hers for a long wonderful moment.

"Goodnight, Samuel. The first of many, I hope" and her lips covered his for a longer moment.

" '*They say that hope is happiness*', " he quoted and assumed she wouldn't know the ending of that Byron poem, and the thought of it gave him a brief shudder.

> (*Alas! It is delusion all.*
> *The future cheats us from afar.*
> *Nor can we be what we recall,*
> *Nor dare we think on what we are.*)

But his lips were covering hers again and nothing else really mattered. So Lord Byron was left for another day and Ms. Reynard waived her six date rule and Judge Blaine need not have worried about Senator Dole nor his syndrome and the guest bedroom the next morning was as neat as it had been when they had arrived.

"Debbie, old girl, you make one fine cup of coffee and I sure would appreciate another," requested Bull Heimlich and Debbie Budoniak shot him a side-long glance but went fetching for a refill anyway, but not for the boss. Jack was a liberated man and got his own coffee.

"What do you hear from Whelan?" asked Jack.

"Not a thing. He hasn't kept touch with anyone for weeks now. His disciplinary hearing has been postponed till January. His wife has called looking for him a few times, probably late on his child support check. They tell me he's been drinking a lot."

"Are you surprised? He hasn't exactly got a lot to show for himself these days. Broken hearts are hard to mend." Jack felt a lonesome country song coming on, but let it pass out of respect for his secretary.

"What is it with you men that you let any woman who comes along manipulate you?" asked Debbie scornfully.

"Sometimes we just don't see things the way they are," offered Jack.

"Sometimes we just like being manipulated," claimed Bull. "Personally, if they want to manipulate me and pretend they're in love, for the sake of avoiding an unpleasant scene, I'm willing to let them pretend. But say, Deb, you're not pretending with me, now, are ya?"

"Bull, I think you're a disgusting pig, and I'm really not pretending about that."

"Hey, that's cool. I can live with that. You're pretty close to the truth there," and he threw her a wink and she couldn't help laughing through her frustration.

"One of these days your wife is going to throw you right out on your ear," she rebuked.

"Wouldn't surprise me. And I wouldn't blame her," said Bull.

Debbie made some kind of unintelligible choking, pre-expectorating sound and vanished into the outer office.

Jack mused. "What is it about cops? You guys seem to have the highest divorce rate of any profession."

"Not an easy job," said Bull. "High tension, easy temptation, always someone out there trying to shag a guy in uniform. Mostly, though, I think it's just that empty feeling you get on the job."

"What do you mean?"

"Well, Jack, what time of day do people usually need a cop?"

"At night, I suppose."

"Right. The day shift guys are pretty much putting in their time until retirement, doing bank escorts, directing traffic, making sure the school crossing guards show up. It's the second and third shift guys do most of the work. That's when most normal people are at home. Let me tell ya, it ain't easy driving around in a patrol car at night and seeing all the lights on in normal homes with normal people sitting around their televisions or having dinner together or watching the dads playing with their kids or young couples coming home from the movies. Then the next thing you know you're putting your life on the line because some worthless piece of shit gets into an argument with some other worthless piece of shit over some other worthless piece of shit. Then before you know it your kids are all grown up and having their own problems and you realize you hardly ever had a chance to meet them. So you start feeling sorry for yourself and that's the worst thing you can do, Jack, the WORST THING, because that leaves you wide open and vulnerable to the first piece of shit that comes along with a plan to change your life for the better, and you figure, how much worse could it get? But somehow, somehow it always does."

"You know what, Bull? I think Debbie likes you."

"Yeah, I can tell."

Perhaps it was the glow of new love, but the usually hard-hearted Samuel Blaine found himself deeply moved by the probation report on Daisy Nichols. The Beatrice Hurley letter was included, and a summary of the Family Court record of her youth. *Yeah, we sure did a good job with her. Surprise, surprise. She graduated from the system and still has some issues.*

In addition to the probation report, the judge had ordered a transcript of the trial and spent most of the next few days reading it over very carefully. Lynn had suggested that they should avoid contact until the sentencing on December 3rd, so he had the usual large amounts of free time on his hands, which he spent thinking of her and working on a couple of sonnets.

Maybe you can't change the past, he thought. *But maybe, just maybe it's possible to start over. Maybe there's still time for happiness.*

As they did every December 3rd, the family Hughes attended the 6:45 a.m. Mass at St. Mary's. For Neil's family, that meant leaving the house by 6, a huge sacrifice, but one they made without grumbling. As they knelt together again in the first two pews of the dim church, they remembered him, a man the children had never met.

December 3, 1974, 06:00.

The sharp ring of the old rotary phone in the hall pierces the early morning. Mom reaches the phone first as Neil stands dazed outside his door. "Hello?. . .Yes. Yes.. . .When?. . .O.K.. ..Thank you. . . .Riley's. ..O.K."

Riley's is the family funeral parlor. Neil knows immediately that Dad's five year struggle for life is ended. He was 52.

She turns to Neil and says, "Well, it's over."

They quietly make their way downstairs to the kitchen. It is so very dark and so very still. Eight-year-old brother Jack remains asleep upstairs. Two of the other kids are away at college and a third in the army somewhere in Alabama. Neil puts a pot of water on for tea, but Mom will have none. Ever practical, she ignores her grief to begin to plan for all the little things that will need to be done over the next several days. The Red Cross will find Eddie and arrange for a flight home. Ultimately the burden of breaking the news to the college siblings will fall on Neil.

He suddenly realizes that the dress rehearsal for a community benefit performance of Damn Yankees *is that evening. He does some quick calculating and realizes that if the funeral is two days hence, they can bury Dad in the morning and he can still be ready to open the show that night.*

Last night he hadn't gone to see Dad at the hospital and went to rehearsal instead.

After all, he had been in the hospital twenty or thirty times in the last five years.

When Damn Yankees *closed he would never step foot on a stage again.*

A couple of hours later, little Jack is sitting in the bathtub. He looks up at Neil.

"Neil, did you hear about Dad?"

"Yes. . . . I did."

Twenty-five years. Could it really be that long?

This was the parish of their immigrant great-great grandparents and their numerous progeny, where Dad had been baptized, confirmed and buried. He had tagged along with his older sister when she started in the parish school and found himself admitted a year early, ultimately graduating Salutatorian of the class of '39.

In February of 1934, in one of the coldest spells of the century, his father, racked with fever, begged him to open the windows. He died soon after at 41. The family ice business went down the tubes and their grandmother struggled for the rest of her life.

On his deathbed their grandfather had made her promise that no matter what happened she would keep the kids in St. Mary's. She did.

No chance for college, of course, till the War and the GI Bill intervened. By the time he passed the bar exam in the early 1950's his heart condition had become obvious and he had the first of three major operations with four children under the age of 6. Each time his career advanced, his health worsened and knocked him back.

But he always had time to be Dad. Neil would never forget the night they went to Fenway Park to see Ted Williams play in his last season, a favor Neil would return years later by plopping two-year-old Neil, Jr. on his shoulders to get a close-up view of The Splendid Splinter in Cooperstown on Induction Day at the Hall of Fame.

And Neil remembered the last game of the 1960 World Series, sitting with Dad in their 1957 Ford Station Wagon in front of the Sanford Mills Post

Office, listening on the car radio as Bill Mazeroski parked the homer in the bottom of the ninth to win the Series for Pittsburgh.

And he taught his children about Normandy and the War and talked politics with Neil, the only one of them expressing much of an interest, telling him about Robert Taft, and Bill Knowland, and Douglas MacArthur, and William F. Buckley, Jr. and Barry Goldwater and *National Review*.

And in October of 1964 he handed 13-year-old Neil a phone book and said, "You've got the K's. Call everybody and tell them to watch Channel 6 tonight at 7:00. Ronald Reagan will be discussing the issues." At the time Neil had no idea who Ronald Reagan was, other than vaguely. That night and The Speech would fix him as an icon forever.

Dad ran for office only once, for the Sanford Mills City Council. He lost by seven votes. The conventional wisdom had it that he was too conservative to get elected. When told of this, he remarked, "I had no idea there was an ideology for removing snow."

So, when Dad died Neil finally began to think for the first time about Law School, and in a sense he was trying to complete his work, to do all those many things Dad would have done had he been able, including dabbling in politics. Dad would have been most proud to watch his son cast a vote at the 1980 Republican National Convention for Reagan.

"Your father was the most stubborn and pig-headed man I ever met," an aging politician had once told Neil.

"That's what I liked about him. He had convictions."

That he did.

The Mass was for the feast of St. Francis Xavier. The family had for a quarter of a century marveled that God had chosen that feast day to welcome home his good and faithful servant Francis J. Hughes.

"Remember Francis. In Baptism he died with Christ. May he also share in his Resurrection," intoned the priest.

"Amen," whispered Neil.

"Amen," whispered Jack.

Chapter 18.

Once again, the public's interest in the Daisy Nichols case had waned. Not even the usual reporter was present for sentencing, she having made a previous arrangement to call in for the final result.

The defendant entered the courtroom with head bowed, handcuffed and sporting leg shackles and the standard issue orange jail jumpsuit instead of the neat civilian clothes she had worn throughout the trial. No need to pretend any more since the jury had been discharged.

Judge Blaine took the bench quickly.

"Have both sides had an opportunity to review the probation report?"

"We have, your honor," replied Ms. Reynard.

"We have, also," said the District Attorney.

"Before we proceed to sentencing, are there any post-trial motions for the People?" inquired the Judge.

"No thank-you," said the District Attorney.

"Anything for the Defendant?"

"Your honor, on behalf of the Defendant, Daisy Nichols, I would renew my motion for a directed verdict and move to set aside the verdict of the jury on the grounds that as a matter of law the People failed to prove each and every element of each and every charge beyond a reasonable doubt," tried Attorney Reynard, with an eye to preserving the record.

"Do the People wish to be heard on the motion?"

"Briefly, your honor. The evidence presented supported the charges, the jury deliberated at great length and clearly gave careful attention to your instructions and the evidence and made a determination that no one could say is unreasonable. Therefore the motion should be denied and the verdict sustained. Thank you," concluded the District Attorney.

Judge Blaine looked around the courtroom, then at the District Attorney, the Defendant and the Defense Attorney.

"I have had an opportunity to examine the transcripts of the trial, and of course I have been actively involved with every stage of these proceedings and indeed have had the same opportunity as the jurors to observe the credibility and demeanor of the witnesses in this case. In order for the Court to grant the motion to set aside the verdict I would need to find that as a matter of law no reasonable person could examine the evidence presented and return a verdict of guilty. I would have to make such a finding in the face of a verdict separately and unanimously reached by twelve good people of this county. It should come as no surprise that courts are exceptionally reluctant to make such determinations, and there are wise and sound reasons for courts to affirm jury verdicts. It helps retain public confidence in the judicial system and provides continuity with a long line of justice reaching back into the very mists of time.

"It may, therefore, come as a surprise to you that I intend to grant the motion in part and deny it in part."

There was momentary confusion. Daisy looked up for the first time, puzzled. The District Attorney was starting to get extremely agitated and Lynn Reynard looked on Samuel with profound surprise and sudden admiration.

Judge Blaine continued. "The lesser included charge of Assault in the Second Degree relating to the defendant punching the deceased in the head and drawing substantial amounts of blood is amply supported by the record and her own admissions to Marie Daley and will be sustained. The other assault charges, burglary charges and the charge of Murder in the Second Degree are not so supported beyond a reasonable doubt and will be dismissed.

"As I have indicated, I do not make this decision lightly, but after a great deal of soul-searching and a careful review of the record. And save your breath, Mr. District Attorney, your exception is duly noted and preserved and of course the People have a right to appeal this judgment, and I assume you will.

"On the only remaining charge of Assault Second, does the defendant know of any reason why sentence should not be pronounced at this time?"

"No, your honor," beamed Lynn Reynard.

"Do the People know of any reason?"

The District Attorney was speechless, grasping for anything, but coming up short. Finally he stood.

"Judge, this is totally outrageous. How can you do this? This is a violation of your oath of office and a slap in the face to the people of this county. You are handing the criminals of this county a license to kill."

The old Judge Blaine might have turned white with rage. The new judge simply sighed.

"I thoroughly understand your frustration, sir, and am obligated to remind you of the sanctions available for contempt of court. Please answer the question: do you know of any reason sentence should not be pronounced."

"Yes," said the District Attorney. "I move that sentencing be delayed until we have had an opportunity to appeal to the Appellate Division of the Third

Department."

"Denied. We will proceed to sentence."

Daisy Nichols, still not comprehending, stood with her attorney.

"Ms. Reynard, do you wish to be heard?"

"Thank you. The defendant has been in jail since March, more than eight months. The major charges have been dismissed. I think she should be released based on her prior history and her already lengthy incarceration, which would be the equivalent of better than a year sentence with good behavior."

"Ms. Nichols, do you wish to be heard?" Daisy shook her head.

"Do the People wish to be heard?"

"The People are opposed to any release of the Defendant and request the maximum sentence allowed by law," and held his tongue for now, though his knuckles had turned very, very white while his hands grasped the edges of the prosecutor's table.

"Daisy Nichols, upon conviction of the crime of Assault in the Second Degree, a Class D Felony, it is the judgment of this Court that you be sentenced to time served. The Sheriff is directed to release you from custody immediately. Ms. Nichols, you have a right to be heard after sentencing. Is there anything you'd like to say at this time?"

Tears streamed down her face. "Yes. Thank you. Thank you."

And as quickly as he had entered the courtroom he just as quickly left, leaving a baffled staff, a stunned District Attorney, and Lynn Reynard hugging her client, the two of them jumping up and down like a couple of bobbysoxers.

It was a Friday. Publishing deadlines for local papers being what they were, the news didn't trickle out till the Monday editions, but then the public got interested quickly.

Sanford Mills' only radio station, serving the greater Sanford Mills community in exactly the same way for half a century, provided a daily outlet for citizen frustration: *Speak Soundly*, a listener call-in show hosted by the ever-affable Cuddy Bradmore, heard right after the 10:45 Obituaries.

"Good morning, Cuddy, how are you?"

"Well, good morning, Cinderella. Got anything on your mind today?"

"I'll say I do. What's with this Judge Blaine. Has he gone out of his mind? I say if somebody murders somebody they should be put to death! Immediately! Instead this guy just gives her a slap on the wrist and then lets her go! I tell you, Cuddy, this really makes me mad!"

"Have you been following the trial in the paper?"

" I don't believe anything I read in that paper. All I know is the police arrested her for murder and now she's walking the streets!"

"Well, Cinderella, I don't know too much about it yet, but from what I understand the Judge found the evidence was insufficient to convict her. Doesn't that mean she's not guilty?"

"What it means is that these wacko judges are getting soft in the head! The criminals are getting more rights than the citizens!"

"OK, well, thanks for your thoughts Cinderella, and you have a good day. The phone lines are all lit up and I see we have Roger-Dodger on line two. How ya doing there Roger?"

"I tell you what, Cuddy. I think I know what happened here. The District Attorney screwed up. Sam Blaine is no wacko judge. When he was District Attorney, the criminals ended up behind bars where they belong! He wouldn't just let somebody go unless they were really not guilty. I know that for a fact!"

"All right, well we certainly have some divergent opinions here. Let's see what Lilith has to say. Good morning, Lilith!"

" I know one of the jurors, Cuddy, and you know what she told me? She said that the defense attorney was some good-looking blonde from out of town! You know what I think happened? I think that judge took one look at her and decided . . ."

What followed was a brief musical interlude and the station jingle.

"Now Lilith, you know the rules. No attacks of a personal nature and some of those words you know we can't put on the air. That's why we have that ten-second delay. I'm afraid we're going to have to put you on the Time-Out list for two weeks. Sorry. Next up in the queue we have Stubborn-Old-Alice. Alice, are you ready to *Speak Soundly?*"

"Cuddy, I don't like what you just did to Lilith. That's not fair. She has a right to express her opinion! This is our show and you shouldn't be censoring it!"

"Well, actually, Alice, we are regulated by the FCC and technically, I think, the show really belongs to the sponsors."

"See, that's what I'm talking about. The federal government keeps sticking its nose where it don't belong, trying to regulate our right of free speech! And who are these sponsors? Maybe we could start a boycott or something," she cackled.

"Maybe this would be a good time to take our first commercial break. This is Cuddy Bradmore mike-side and we'll be right back with more of *Speak Soundly.*"

At which point he skipped over the primary sponsor's ad and slipped in one for the plumber who had left a mess and overcharged him the week before.

Attorney Reynard and former Defendant Daisy Nichols had lunch together in freedom on Monday in an upscale restaurant in Bath Springs, Lynn's treat. Afterwards they hung around the yuppie bar for a good part of the afternoon, sampling a variety of the micro-brews produced on premises.

"You know, Daisy, you don't have to live in the past."

"What do you mean?"

"I'm talking about the child abuse. It wasn't your fault, any of it."

"I know that, I guess," said Daisy quietly.

"Daisy, I've been there."

Daisy stared at her lawyer in disbelief. This beautiful, self-assured, successful attorney, brimming with confidence, abused? *I don't think so.*

"It messed me up for a while. It really did. But I dealt with it. And I got over it and moved on. In my case it was sexual abuse, not physical, but that shouldn't make a difference. Abuse is abuse."

Daisy recoiled at the memory of her "father" and felt real uncomfortable about her brother.

"You? I don't believe it," Daisy said.

"Believe it. While my mother was alive, I really couldn't do anything about it. I didn't want to cause trouble in the family. But my therapist said that it's important to confront the person who abused you and let them know how you feel about it. As soon as my mother was gone, that's exactly what I did. You've got to just lay it all on them and that helps lift the burden off yourself. You should try it."

"I could never be like you," said Daisy.

"Sure you could. You just have to work at it. We'll start right now. We'll go to the beauty parlor and do a complete make-over. New hairstyle, a nail job, get you some makeup and teach you how to use it. Not much we can do with the tattoos, but hey, they're in style now. I've got some clothes that should fit you. A little conservative jewelry. Have you ever considered getting your belly-button pierced?"

A plain envelope arrived addressed to Miss Lynn Reynard. Inside she found a single sheet of paper containing a title and fourteen lines of rhymed iambic pentameter, though she surely did not recognize it as such.

Pygmalion's Folly

A lifetime have I labored at my stone —
No time to live, to love or to regret.
I choose not now to think myself alone,
But tap away with chisel lightly set
To bring forth every nuance, every line
Of ideal womanhood. Of course I know
That such a creature never could be mine,
So wonderful and fair, yet even so
I chip away, quite madly, to create
A glorious vision men will all adore:
The perfect image of the perfect mate,
Outshining every one made heretofore!

And yet, before I finished, in you came —
And all my dreams and visions put to shame.

-S.R. Poeta
12/5/99

I think he likes me. I think he really likes me!

Samuel began spending more and more time in Bath Springs, always arriving late and leaving early so no one would find out. He used the car without the judicial plates and parked it in her private area where it could not be seen from the street. No one knew about them. No one at all.

Except the one who was watching.

Night after night after night.

Chapter 19.

It was a week before Christmas. Jack was in his easy chair reading the evening paper. Jack, Jr. was lying on a blanket on his back, trying to turn over. Laura, doll in hand, paraded around the living room, occasionally stopping to do a little dance for the baby, or play little piggies on his toes. Maria sat at her desk going through the day's mail.

"Here's a card from your Aunt Gertie. She says they're going to Florida for a couple of months."

"Mmph," said Jack.

"Oh, and here's one from my freshman roommate! Guess I have to send *her* one now."

"Ynnhh," agreed Jack.

"Your California nephews are certainly getting big. We should go out and see them."

"Ahyrrnt," commented Jack.

"And here's one for you from Gold Harbor. The Sullivans."

"Let me see that," said Jack, jumping from his chair.

"Laura, look! Daddy's alive!"

Laura ran into her father's arms and gave him a big hug.

The card had a note with a newspaper clipping inside.

> *Dear Jack and Family,*
> *All the best for the holidays and thanks again for all you did.*
> *We had a marvelous time at Faith's class reunion! Enclosed is*
> *a copy of the newspaper clipping about the reunion. They*
> *insisted we pose for the picture, too! What nice kids!*
> *Love,*
> *Mike and Genevieve*

"Gee, that's great," said Jack, showing it to Maria.

"Chalk one up for good deeds," said Maria. "I'm really happy for them."

The clipping slipped to the floor. Jack picked it up and returned to his chair before opening it. It was from the Thursday edition of the *Gold Harbor*

Gazette, a big class photo under the headline **"McClure Class of '69 Holds Thirtieth Reunion"**. Jack smiled as he found Mike and Genevieve kneeling in the front row.

Then he saw something else.

"Oh, my God," he said slowly.

"Oh, my God. Oh, my God."

"Ho-ly shit!" said Bull Heimlich when Jack showed him the picture. "Holy freakin' shit!"

"That's what *I* said. Sort of."

"What do we do with this?"

"I think we have to show our bosses," said Jack.

Within half an hour they had gathered at Sheriff Rushmore's house.

"So what's this about, Jack?" asked the District Attorney.

Jack handed him the picture. The Sheriff looked over his shoulder.

There in the second row of the Bishop McClure class of 1969 stood Judge Samuel R. Blaine with his arm around Ms. Lynn Reynard.

"How did you get this," asked the Sheriff. So Jack once again told the story about the class ring in the case at the Inn and the moon paper and Faith Sullivan and the cliff and Mike and Genevieve.

And then a terrible thought hit him.

"This Lynn Reynard. She looks an awful lot like the dead girl."

"So? She's the wrong age, can't be related too closely and probably not at all," said the Sheriff.

"Still, there's something about that girl's death that has been troubling me," said Jack, who was glad Bull didn't say anything just then. "Just out of curiosity, I'd like to make a phone call."

"Mike, this is Jack Hughes. We got your card today."

They exchanged pleasantries.

"Mike, the reason I'm calling, and this may seem odd to you, but trust me that I have a good reason for asking, I need to know who was with Faith the day she died?"

"That is an odd request," said Mike, slowly. "But I certainly trust your judgment. It was Sammy Blaine. You might have heard of him. I hear he's a judge somewhere up your way."

"Yeah, I know him all right. Listen, Mike, it might be better if you don't tell Genevieve about this, ok?"

"What's this about, Jack?"

"Probably nothing. But I need to know what I'm dealing with. Thanks, Mike."

"I'll tell you, Jack, he sure looked like he was head over heels in love with that girl he took to the reunion. Everyone said so. He, uh, he never came over to say hello. . . . He was the only one. . . . Goodnight, Jack. Good luck."

"Goodnight, Mike."

Once again Mike Sullivan felt very, very old.

"OK," said the District Attorney. "Suppose he did kill that girl when he was 18. What's that to us? You're not suggesting that we reopen a thirty-year-old murder in another county in another state, are you?"

"I guess not," said Jack. "But where does that leave us?"

"Well, I think the Commission on Judicial Conduct needs to be informed. And I think we need to conduct our own investigation so we have something to present to the Appellate Division on the appeal. I'm afraid someone is going to have to interview Lynn Reynard. If they were an item before he granted that motion, or even before the trial, we have a right to know that. I still can't believe it."

Jack showed the picture to the District Attorney again. "Believe it."

"Well then," said the District Attorney, how the heck do we get Ms. Reynard to cooperate? She's as slick as they come. She'll never help us."

"There is a way," said the Sheriff.

"What's that?" asked the District Attorney.

"The Heimlich Maneuver."

"Hello. This is Lynn Reynard."

"Yo, Lynn! This is Bull. What's happenin'?"

Lynn smiled. "What happened to all that ma'am stuff?"

"Hey, trial's over and after that one you ain't likely to get too many more assignments in DeWitt County, know what I'm sayin'? So I figure it's safe to call you Lynn for a while."

"I'm honored. And just what is the purpose of your call?"

"Nothin' much. Just wonderin' if you might be free for lunch sometime."

"Bull Heimlich, I have a certain ethical code, and the number one rule is *Don't Date Married Men*."

"Hey, I'm not talkin' about a *date*. Just a little friendly get-together. No obligations. Whadya say?"

"Why do I have the feeling that certain obligations might come creeping into this anyway? Alright, as long as it's not a date. We'll call it an un-date."

The following noon they were un-dating for lunch in a neutral county.

"So, Lynn, how come you're not married?" he thrust.

"How come you are?" she parried.

"Touché," he said, not meaning it.

She laughed, delightfully, with just a shade of intimacy.

"Well, since you're so curious, Bull, I *was* married, once, for about four years. I decided I disliked very much being possessed, and determined never to be possessed again. So I just don't get involved."

"Still you're awful pretty. Seems like such a waste."

"I work at it. I believe a person should always try to look and be their very best. Some people think that makes me vain. Do you think I'm vain?"

"I think the word I'd use is 'classy'," flattered Bull. It was the right thing to say.

"Well, I think it takes a pretty classy man to recognize classy, Bull Heimlich."

"Yeah, I've been called that."

Lunch arrived. Both ate well.

"So, I gather that *L.A. Confidential* is your favorite movie," offered Bull as the plates were removed.

"What do you mean?"

"All that 'Call me Lynn' stuff. Straight out of the picture."

She gave him a sly, conspiratorial smile. "I *hated* it. One of the stupidest movies I've ever seen."

Bull raised an eyebrow as the coffee arrived. He stirred his cup, though he hadn't put anything in it.

"Now, Lynn, are things all over between you and Whelan or are you still carrying a torch?"

She looked hurt, and said quietly, "Bull, there was never anything at all between me and Whelan. He was having problems with his wife and I listened to him a bit. Maybe I was too kind." *That can't be it,* thought Bull. "I never led him on, but then he starts following me around and acting all goofy like he's in love or something. He's really a sick, sick person."

"Yeah, well he was never one of my favorite people. Too bad, though. He might lose his job."

"That's no concern of mine," said Ms. Reynard, matter-of-factly. "I hope that's not why you're here, because I have no intention of covering up for him. He'll get what he deserves."

"Nah, that's not why I'm here. *This* is why I'm here," and he laid the photograph on the table in front of her.

She turned pale and frosty.

-130-

"Where did you get this?" she demanded.

"Did I mention I like to go scuba diving? Great sport. My favorite spot is right off the beach in Gold Harbor, Maine. Sometimes I even pick up the local paper while I'm there. Pretty amazing what you can find there, wouldn't you say?"

"Who else knows about this?"

"Just my scuba partner, a fella named Jack Hughes."

She calculated. No point in denial.

"Bull, I swear to you this was completely innocent. He pressured me to go to that party with him. I figured no one would know. We never discussed the case, at all. There's nothing going on now and there never was. Now *this*," she said tossing the photo back, "can destroy my reputation and my career, and I *didn't do anything wrong!*"

And now she cried.

Bull admired the performance. *She's really very, very good.*

"Hey, Lynn, I believe you," he said. "Why shouldn't I? After all you're a law-yer," and he twinkled at her and the tears stopped. "Law-yers always tell the truth, right?"

"Please don't hold my profession against me."

"There's only one thing I'd like to hold against you, and that's me."

An opening?

"Bull, you won't use this, will you?"

He laughed. "Now there you go, jumpin' to conclusions. Whadya think, everything's about *you*? This ain't about you. It's about *Sam Blaine.*"

"But how can you do anything to him without hurting me? It's not fair. And I certainly won't agree to anything that might prejudice my client."

"Now you're three steps ahead on the wrong track. Maybe I better start over. There was this girl in Sam's class that looked a lot like you."

Lynn was completely bewildered. She made a bewildered face. "OK, Bull, you've got my complete attention."

"She went for a walk with Sam thirty years ago. She never came back." And now Bull related in some detail the story of Faith Sullivan and the dark secret of Samuel R. Blaine.

She listened attentively, but was skeptical. "You mean to say the respected, learned, wise and courageous judge of the DeWitt County Court may be at heart a homicidal maniac? That's a little hard to swallow."

"I've asked around," said Bull. "He isn't close to anybody. Lots of professional friends and friendly acquaintances, but the guy is a loner. And the folks in Gold Harbor say he was the same way then. Fact is, *you* are the only person who's gotten anywhere near close to him. Did he say anything or did you hear anything or see anything at the reunion that might shed some light on this?"

She pondered and calculated, calculated and pondered.

"First of all, I repeat, we are not and have not been close. But as for seeing or hearing, there was one thing."

"What's that?"

"He kept this blue spiral notebook from when he was in high school, full of weird poems about unrequited love. I read some of it. I don't much understand poetry, but even for poetry some of it seemed a little strange. I didn't see any specific reference to the Sullivan girl, but there were quite a few poems and they all seemed to be about different women, and as I say, I didn't read them all."

"Do you know where that notebook is now?" asked Bull.

"Sure. He put it back in his old desk in his old room in his mother's house in Gold Harbor."

"Think you could get it?"

"Think you could keep me out of this if I do?"

"Lynn, Lynn. Knowing the way I feel about you, do you really think there is *any way* that I wouldn't make sure you were treated exactly the way you deserve to be?"

It worked.

"Bull, I think I'm gonna buy you a beer."

"I'd like that."

Bull Heimlich! Now it's that goddam Bull Heimlich!

He continued to watch and seethe as the Acting Undersheriff and the lawyer spent hour after leisurely hour entertaining each other at the bar.

Chapter 20

```
Memo
To: Sheriff
From: W. Heimlich
Re: Blaine/Reynard Investigation
Date: 12/23/99
```
As per your directive I made contact with Ms.
Reynard and confronted her with the evidence of her
trip with the judge. She was a little resistant but
admitted that they had been together but denied
anything improper. At this point she is being
reasonably cooperative. She believes our primary
interest is with respect to the Maine matter and in
that regard I have contacted Investigator Lamont
Keegan of the Gold Harbor P.D. and filled him in.
They are reopening their file. Interestingly,
Reynard believes there may actually be some evidence
at the Blaine homestead in the form of old writings
by S.B. She is willing to take a look on her own.

In that connection she advises that she will
see if the judge will take her home for Christmas to
meet his mother and spend a few days. The courts
will be closed between Christmas and New Year's so
it might happen. If so, I am requesting
authorization to travel there along with ADA Hughes
and Joe Probello (to take advantage of any
interesting photo opportunities).

At this point I don't think we need to worry
about LR spilling the beans to SB. Her primary
interest appears to be self-preservation. Actually,
her only interest. If she has any romantic interest
in the judge she is hiding it real well. She says
he 'pressured' her into going to the class reunion.

I'm no psychologist, but I find her a little
scary. She can be smiling away at you and be
detached at the same time. She has total control
over the tear ducts and can flip from flirty to

frosty in a split-second.

  I checked with her hometown PD on the q.t.
Was nothing too abnormal about the family. She did
have a somewhat odd older brother who disappeared a
few years ago after the mother died, but no one in
the family seemed too concerned about it.

  Have attempted to get hold of Whelan to see
what he has to add, but can't find him. Never
answers phone. I've left six messages and driven to
his place twice but can't catch him. Mail is being
picked up so he must be around. Will keep trying.
WH

  "Do you love me, Samuel? Do you really love me?"

  Sam Blaine looked down at his slightly inebriated friend and said, sincerely, "Yes, Lynn. I really love you."

  "Do you really, really, really, really love me?"

  "I really, really, really, really, really love you."

  "Wow. Five reallys!" She snuggled closer. "Take me away. Let's go somewhere where we can be alone together without worrying about who's watching."

  "Where would you like to go?" asked Sam.

  "Why don't we go back to Gold Harbor for Christmas? I could meet your mother."

  "Sorry, Lynn. Mom's off to Florida for the season."

  She gave him a devilish grin. "Then we could have the whole house to ourselves!"

  He liked the idea. Very much.

  "One more thing, Samuel," she cooed. "Do you really, really, really, really, really, really love me?"

  At 4 a.m. on December 24, Judge Blaine arrived with his big Judge-mobile to quietly pick up Lynn Reynard and her several travel bags, sure that no one would notice them at that hour, and no one did except Joe Probello with his long lens, and the other one.

  Joe Probello! What the heck is he doing here? And now Whelan Oates was not only possessed, but curious, as three cars on the same block all started off for Gold Harbor, Maine.

  Jack Hughes absolutely refused to spend Christmas away from his family and Bull had some domestic obligations of his own, so Joe Probello served as advance picket and even managed to find a B&B right across the street from the Blaine house. From there he viewed the comings and goings, though the couple rarely left the house until dinner time, and then only for a few hours. He had enough shots of them together to cause an average blackmailer to salivate, but Joe was perfectly legit and in this for the sport. At night only one bedroom light went on, and only one went off.

Bull and Jack checked into the Gold Harbor Beach Inn on December 27 and got an update from Probello. They remained in cell-phone contact with him at all times so they could move relatively freely about town without worrying about being seen by the judge just yet. This enabled them to make a few trips to the one-hour photo developing niche in the department store out on the highway, and to touch bases with Lamont Keegan. Otherwise, they just waited to hear from Lynn Reynard.

"Oh, Samuel, isn't this wonderful? I would just LOVE to wake up every morning in your arms," she proclaimed on the morning of December 30.

"I gotta tell you, Lynn, if we didn't have to worry about that other stuff there would be nothing in the world that would keep me away from you."

"You know, why should we give a crap what other people think. *I love you, you love me, let's go kiss behind that tree,*" she sang in mock-rendition of that revolting purple dinosaur song.

"I wish it could be that easy," he said seriously, and kissed her, tree or no tree.

He heard his cell phone ring in his sport-coat pocket in the dining room downstairs.

He sighed. "I'd better check that out. Only my secretary has the number and I told her only to call if it was really important."

"I'll be waiting for you!" she called after him brightly.

As soon as the he left she closed the door and retrieved the spiral notebook from the desk drawer. She plowed through it as quickly as possible.

Looks like he got turned down four times for the Junior Prom. I wonder what was wrong with him. I had fun at the Junior Prom. What was that guy's name?

Then she found the one dated July 22, 1969.

Then she read it.

Then she tore it out and put it in her purse.

"This better be good, Doris. I'm on vacation."

"Judge, I hope you're sitting down and I hope you're alone."

He closed the door. He sat down.

-135-

"Go ahead," said Judge Blaine.

"You are definitely not going to want to hear this. I just got a call from the Judicial Conduct Commission. They're investigating you."

"Who's complaining now?" he asked, impatiently, knowing that disgruntled criminal defendants often find themselves time to whine about their judges while twiddling away their sentences.

"Lynn Reynard."

And suddenly Cloud Nine came crashing down to earth at warp speed.

"Lynn Reynard? Are you kidding?"

"I'll tell you exactly what they asked me. They wanted to know if I knew anything about you taking a trip with her Thanksgiving weekend and if I knew anything about your sexually harassing her or any other female attorneys or staff."

"This is absolutely ridiculous," said Judge Blaine.

"That's what I said. Then they told me that Lynn has already admitted going with you and that you pressured her and that she felt that she had no choice but to do whatever you wanted her to, that she was afraid that if she didn't neither she nor her clients would ever get a fair shake from you."

"This is so preposterous. What did you tell them?"

"I said, 'Sexual Harassment is not a problem in this office. It's one of the benefits.'"

"I hope you're making a joke," urged the judge.

Doris laughed. "Yeah, I made that part up. Don't worry, boss. No one will ever believe her."

"What makes you say that?"

"Everyone knows what she is. She'll do and say anything to get what she wants. That's pretty obvious. People see right through her. She uses men and throws them away like facial tissue. Look what she did to Whelan Oates."

Judge Blaine was out of the loop. "What did she do to him?"

"Boy, you really are in another world." And so she told him the Whelan Oates story via the Courthouse Gossip Network. He was, to say the least, stunned.

"Sorry to have to break up your holiday with this, but I thought you should know. Well, hey, there's a new millennium coming. Have you got a date for New Year's?" she asked.

"No. Not at the moment," said the judge. "Goodbye. And thank you. For everything."

After they hung up he stared at the phone for a long time.

Just like the others.

-136-

"Samuel," she said after they made love for the last time, "let's go into town today. I'd like to do a little shopping and stop at the stationery store so I can fax some stuff to my office. We sole practitioners don't have the luxury of total relaxation on vacations, you know."

"I remember," he said. "That's why I became a judge."

"And such a terrific judge, too," she exclaimed, giving him a playful squeeze.

There would always be a certain sadness when he thought of her, he knew. She had made that wonderful fantasy very, very real for him, and he had been happier than he'd been in years. Happier than he'd *ever* been, maybe. Even if this had all been a fraud for her, the emotions he had felt had been no less real. And although she obviously made a lousy life partner, she had been one terrific date.

Yes, he would miss her.

Sometimes, even now, he missed the other one, too.

"Tell you what, darling. After you finish your errands we'll go for a nature walk. The dunes and hills are wildly beautiful in December. Just like you."

He smiled at her.

She curled into his arms.

"I love you!" she said.

"I love you, too," he replied.

Whoever you are.

Chapter 21.

Well, at least they were here on an expense account. Jack sifted through the display in the lobby again, wondering whatever had possessed him to look at that ring in the first place, that little class ring that had set all these events in motion.

There were those dog tags, hanging where they had been, another mystery waiting to be solved.

No thanks.

"So, Bull, do you think there's a devil?" asked Jack, anticipating a somewhat different perspective from his brother's.

"Well, I believe in the Bogeyman, and I know you can't kill the Bogeyman."

"And how do you know that?"

"Because they said so in that movie *Halloween.*"

"Bull, do you know *why* they said that in *Halloween*?"

"No, why?"

"So there'd be a SEQUEL, you jerk!"

Mike Sullivan entered the lobby.

"Mike! What are you doing here?" asked Jack.

"Called your house. Your wife told me where you were, so I thought I'd stop by to say hello."

Jack introduced Mike to Bull.

"That's quite a clever friend you have there, Bull," said Mike. "He's great at solving mysteries."

"Yeah, that's what they say," said Bull. "Does it without any help, too."

"Jack, I've been thinking about your phone call, and I know you've been talking to Lamont. Is there anything you'd like to tell me yet?"

Jack looked at the sad eyes of Mike Sullivan.

"Not yet, Mike. Maybe . . . maybe never."

"I think I have a right to know."

"Mike, really, right now we don't know anything, but we're waiting for something to happen that may not happen. You and your wife have been hurt so much already, I just don't want to set you up for . . . well, you know."

"Yeah. I know."

"Hey. Bull!" yelled Sally O'Brien from across the lobby, "Got a fax here for ya!"

Bull read the paper, whistled and handed it to Jack, who read it, looked at Bull for approval, and handed it to Mike.

And so you slipped the surly bonds of earth
And I alone stood by to watch your flight.
I thought about your ending and your worth
As fitfully I tossed near sleep that night.
It's not that you were wicked, lovely thing.
It's just that you were never quite as good
As I . . .had once supposed. 'Twas just a fling
For you.
　　　　　And so I flung you as I could.
Oh, torture would be better, this I know,
In payment for the pain you've given me.
But I could never, ever stoop so low
As mere revenge.　A sadist I can't be.
And so I tossed you gently in the bay,
And all my nightmares swiftly washed away.

S.R. Poeta
7/22/69

"What does this mean?" asked Mike.

"It means," said Bull, "that the Honorable Samuel R. Blaine, County Court Judge of DeWitt County, New York, Hear Ye, Hear Ye, All Rise in Honor of the Court . . . murdered your daughter."

"But how . . . how did you get this?"

"His girlfriend, Lynn Reynard, is in the house with him. She must have found a way to fax this here."

"He's not at the house," said Mike.

"Well, now how do you know that?" asked Bull.

"I saw his car on the way over here, at least I think it must be his. Big sedan with New York County Judge plates on it. It was in the parking lot up on the hill, by where . . .oh, my God!"

"What?"

"It's where you park to go out by the cliffs where he . . . where he killed my daughter."

A stiff breeze was blowing in. It was mid-day, but the sky was darkening rapidly. There had been very little snow so far this year, but this looked like a big one brewing. Lynn wore a stocking cap, but otherwise let the wind whip through her hair in wild abandon.

"Don't you love it, Lynn? Can you feel it? Can you feel it just wrap right around you the. . .the. . . the PASSION of the UNIVERSE?"

"Oh, I feel it. I FEEL IT!" she shouted above the roar of the wind and the rising surf.

They came across a weather-beaten sign.

WARNING!
DANGEROUS CLIFFS!
NO ONE MAY PASS BEYOND THIS POINT
UNDER PENALTY OF LAW
FINE $50
Gold Harbor Town Council Ordinance 4-1969

"Well, Lynn, I've got two fifties. Do we feel DARING and DANGEROUS and willing to FLAUNT THE LAW?"

"Let's do it!"

So they dashed past the old sign and climbed upward to the edge of the cliff. The surf raged against the rocks far below. He put his arm around her and held her close.

"Do you have any idea how much I have loved you?" he said in her ear.

"I believe I do!" she said in his ear.

"I believe you don't! Otherwise, darling, why would you betray me?"

The three of them sped through Gold Harbor and up the hill in Mike Sullivan's car. The small lot already had two cars in it. Mike ran ahead of the others up the trail, but this was not 1944 and not Normandy and he began to run out of steam just as he spotted them struggling on the edge of the cliff.

"The son-of-a-bitch is doing it again!" he shouted, but he had nothing left and Jack flew by him yelling "STOP!"

But no one could hear him now and he was still 50 yards short of them.

Bull was right behind him, until he saw something else.

Rising from the short underbrush he saw a lone figure raise a revolver and point it straight at the struggling duo.

"WHELAN, YOU STUPID BASTARD!" Bull shouted as he went flying across the headland and with one great leap knocked Whelan Oates over just as the gun went off, harmlessly.

The sound of the discharge caused Sam Blaine to turn and loosen his grip as he took in the whole nightmarish scene. There was . . .Bull Heimlich? . . . struggling with Whelan Oates! . . . Jack Hughes charging at him, and . . .could it be? . . .the father, the FATHER of the other one! *What the hell is happening?*

Which became his final thought as Lynn Reynard, no sixties fair flower but a self-defense-trained woman of the nineties, took advantage of his distraction and deftly flipped Judge Samuel R. Blaine into the abyss.

Jack reached her side.

She threw herself into his arms.

"Oh, Jack! Jack! I was so frightened!"

And she cried.

Bull Heimlich stood over Whelan.

"Whelan Oates, you are one major league asshole! You see this gun, Whelan? Do you see it? Whadja pay for it, three, four hundred bucks? Watch this, Whelan!"

And Bull marched to the cliff and tossed the gun into the ocean.

"And DO NOT, I repeat, DO NOT think you can take up scuba diving so you can get it back, because I AIN'T GONNA TEACH YOU! Now get the HECK out of here and GO HOME! UNDERSTAND?"

Whelan nodded, rose, and made his way down the path.

"I am so glad this is over," she whispered to Jack, being now that close. He recoiled.

"Hold it, lady. This is FAR from over."

"What do you mean?"

"Well, for one thing, you just killed the County Court Judge of DeWitt County, New York. How do you plan on explaining that? Or for that matter, how do you plan on explaining being here?"

"Hey, easy there, Jack. He did try to kill her," interjected Mike.

"Thank you, sir. Do I know you?" asked Lynn.

"Mike Sullivan."

"Oh. Oh!"

Bull looked at her. "Lynn, how do WE know he was trying to kill you. For all we know, *you* could have been trying to kill *him*. All we saw was a struggle. Obviously you are physically capable of killing him, 'cause we saw it with our own eyes."

"What is the MATTER with you people," cried Lynn. "I did nothing wrong!"

"Lynn Reynard, just who the HELL do you think you are?" shouted

Jack, and hoped his mother wasn't listening. "You did nothing wrong? You have done nothing but leave a path of death and destruction wherever you go. You toy with people's emotions. You prey on the vulnerable like the vulture you are. You wreck lives, you destroy marriages, you abandon and betray like it was just some big game. You may have a claim of self-defense, lady, but morally you murdered that man just the same as if you had shot him through the head while he was sleeping."

"THIS IS NOT MY FAULT. NONE OF THIS IS MY FAULT!" she shouted, but even that close they barely heard her, for a great gust of wind like the Wrath of God blew in from the side and knocked Lynn Reynard off balance and over the edge. Jack made a desperate plunge for her, but it was too late.

"I guess I was wrong," Bull remarked as he peered downward. "Maybe you CAN kill the Bogeyman."

When the bodies were recovered three days later, after the storm had subsided, they were found, ironically, together, entwined in a macabre mock-embrace, the same lonely piece of driftwood piercing both their hearts and joining them physically and, perhaps, eternally.

"What happens now?" asked Mike Sullivan.

"Well," said Jack, "I guess we get a hold of Lamont Keegan and tell him what happened."

"Hold it," said Bull. "Mike, we know this guy killed your daughter and now he's dead. Nobody else in the world knows this now but the three of us. Do you want all that brought back up?"

"I'd sooner die myself than put my wife through that agony again."

"Good. Then the poem is out. Agreed?"

The others nodded.

"Whelan, he just plain wasn't here and I'm sure he won't ever say he was. But we still have to explain what the judge and the attorney were doing here together and what WE were doing here. The truth is kinda complicated and a little sticky, and actually a lot sleazy when you get down to it. I think I've got a story will cover it, but it might involve a little truth-stretching. Jack, can you tell a lie?"

"What do you think, Bull?"

"Yeah, well, I didn't think so, but just don't volunteer anything. You take my car and go home. I'll hitch a ride with the photographer and I can start chopping up negatives on the ride back. Meanwhile, Mike, you weren't here. Jack, you weren't here. We'll go back to the Inn and I'll call Lamont from there

after you guys are gone. Deal?"
   "Deal," they replied.

Chapter 22.

Bull had managed to catch up with Whelan, who had been moving none-too-swiftly toward his car, and gently broke the news about Lynn.

"You gonna be alright?"

"Yeah, sure, Bull. It's over. It's finally over."

"Well, get out of town before somebody figures out you're here. Got it?"

"Got it."

The first flakes had already begun to fall before Whelan had even exited Gold Harbor. It was not long before they were coming down steadily, and not long after that treacherously. None of which much mattered to Whelan as he mindlessly drove down the coast road through town after town.

Still, it was slow going and finally as he passed through yet another resort, dead now in the off-season, he spotted a bar that seemed to be open, the *Eight Ball Lounge*. He grimly smiled. *Yeah, that's for me. Behind the eight ball.* He pulled in.

The place seemed a little upscale. A handful of men in small groups, some chattering away, some looking pensive, and several singing along with the juke box, something about a trolley. Sounded like that girl in the *Wizard of Oz*. He struggled for her name. *Judy Manetti or something like that. No, that was her daughter. Judy Garland. That's it.* He slid onto a bar stool.

"Pal, you sure look like you could use one. Rough day?" asked the bartender.

"Yeah, you could say that. This weather ain't helping, either."

"Let me guess," said the bartender. "Leave your lover for a younger model, new lover doesn't last, old lover is gone, and now you are all by yourself alone."

"What are you, some kind of psychic?" asked Whelan in amazement.

"Nah. You'd be surprised how often I hear that story around here. You probably think you're the only one in the world like you sometimes, right?"

"That is true. So there really are others?"

"That's how I stay in business," said the bartender.

"So, why do you call this place the *Eight Ball*? I don't even see a pool table in here."

"Oh, it's a little joke. In season we usually have four bartenders working."

The guys at the juke box were getting a little rowdy as the song reached its climax.

And it was grand just to stand with his hand holding mine . . .
To the end of the line!

"Knock it off, you guys," shouted the bartender. *"Chicago Hope* is coming on."

"You watch *Chicago Hope* reruns?" asked Whelan.

"Well, you can't watch *Northern Exposure* all day. Makes you weird."

"I didn't think anybody watched that show the first time around, let alone reruns."

"Oh, we really like it here. Especially the early ones with Mandy Patinkin. He's very popular with the clientele."

There was a beer in front of him, then another and another and Whelan found himself strangely absorbed in the program. Seems the doctor character likes to sing and his wife who is in a looney home gets him to organize a performance of the psychos. They form a band but can't seem to agree on anything. All kind of self-absorbed. Finally the big day comes and Dr. Mandy, or whatever his name is, performs with them, singing *Casey Would Waltz With a Strawberry Blonde*, or whatever that's called, which must have had something to do with the fact that his wife, the psycho, was also a strawberry blonde, but his name wasn't Casey so it didn't make all that much sense. Then the band comes in real loud, and actually quite good and you can see the psycho wife is delighted and even though she's been looney a long time, the doctor won't get a divorce or date anyone else or anything because he still loves her even though she's nuts and won't do anything for him ever again. She won't even get better for him, the bartender tells him, because she likes being nuts.

It's more than that one song he's singing, it's a medley, the bartender explains, patiently and quietly, because now the whole place is watching and listening.

Once upon a time
A girl with moonlight in her eyes
Put her hand in mine and said she loved me so!
But that was once upon a time
So very long ago.

And for some reason that little song struck Whelan right in the heart and

-146-

he couldn't, just couldn't get it out of his head for the rest of the show and the rest of the beer and the next one and the one after that and even after he had said goodnight to the fellas and they had gone back to the jukebox singing about a boy next door with that Garland woman again.

And now, as he sat in his car in the darkness waiting for the defroster to clear enough of the windshield so he could drive, the song broke up, shattered into tiny little pieces that kept jumping around his brain in all directions. *Once upon a time . . .hand in mine . . .long ago. . .loved me so . . .loved me so . . .said she loved me so . . .moonlight in her eyes . . .her eyes . . .loved me so . . .once upon a time so very long ago. . .*

And now he reached under the seat and felt his fingers grip a metal object, the one Bull didn't know about, the one he kept for emergencies in case anyone ever got the jump on him. *Said she loved me so . . .put her hand in mine . . .but that was once upon a time . . .once upon a time . . .once upon a time never comes again. . .*

He quickly checked to make sure it was loaded. Satisfied, he felt the hum of the engine and the whir of the defroster and there was that girl, that *girl with moonlight in her eyes* while *the band played on* and *his brain was so loaded it nearly exploded* and *once upon a time never comes again. Never. Never. Never. Never.*

His finger tightened around the trigger.
Never comes again.

"Daddy!"

At the sound of his daughter's voice Whelan dropped the gun and turned quickly, wildly in every direction.

But there was no 10-year-old girl there, there couldn't be.

She was half a world away in her home in North Carolina, probably getting ready for bed. Probably saying her prayers.

Did she still say *God bless Daddy*?

And now the semi-frozen windshield wipers broke free with a jerk and in rapid movement began disposing of the accumulated ice and snow and where was she and what was she doing and how did she get here, jumping into my head on a roadside in Maine and God, I miss her. God. I miss her.

And Whelan picked up the gun, carefully emptied it, tossed the rounds in a trash receptacle, returned to his warm cocoon of a vehicle and slowly, but steadily began driving south.

The eastern corridor was a slow crawl, the snow following him for a ways, followed by the traffic tie-ups around the major cities as everyone began gathering to celebrate this unusual New Year, but he doggedly moved forward and more than a full day later arrived on the doorstep of his wife and child.

His wife answered the door.

"Hi," he said.

"What are you doing here?"

"I came to kiss my daughter goodnight."

"Lisa's upstairs. She's already in bed."

"Can I see her?"

She stared at him, then yielded.

"Oh, go on. First door on your right, top of the stairs."

She was asleep.

Whelan leaned over and kissed her gently on the cheek.

"Daddy? Daddy!!"

She hugged him tightly around the neck, so tight her little arms were shaking.

"Daddy! You're home! You're home! Why did you ever leave us?"

And now, at last, came the tears, and the release.

"Lisa, Lisa, Lisa!"

"Don't cry, Daddy. Don't cry!" and now it was the child comforting the parent and Whelan felt more than a little unworthy, and ashamed.

They held each other for a long time until at last she returned to sleep, and Whelan crept silently from her room and saw that his wife had been observing everything from the hall. They went downstairs together. He followed her into the kitchen.

"I am so sorry."

She slapped him across the face.

"Whelan Oates, do you think that after everything you did you can just come flying in here from God-knows where and say I'm sorry and everything's supposed to be ok?"

She slapped him again.

"What are you thinking, Whelan? Do you think that life is just one big Frank Capra movie and all you have to do is get a bunch of people to sing *Auld Lang Syne* and POOF your world is back to normal?"

"It *would* be nice," he said, smiling.

She slapped him again.

"What about *her*?"

"That was over a long time ago. Besides, she never really existed. Besides, she's dead."

"Oh, Whelan! You didn't . . ."

"Nah. Accident. Act of God."

She stared him down some more.

-148-

"Alright, you can stay, but you're not sleeping in my bed," she said at last. "You can sleep in the living room."

"That would be . . .wonderful."

As soon as he settled into the couch, the weeks of sleepless nights came rushing at him and in only a matter of moments he was out cold. His wife hovered over him for a time, shaking her head, and finally went upstairs to her room, climbed into bed and stared at the ceiling.

At 11:55 she crept back downstairs, turned on the television and when the fireworks went off and the horns blew and the people cheered and the bands played *Auld Lang Syne* she woke her husband with a deep, passionate kiss.

Whelan Oates never returned to DeWitt County. He submitted his resignation by mail, collected whatever benefits he had coming to him, and took a job in loss maintenance for a North Carolina department store chain, a job for which he was eminently well-suited. No one ever spoke to him of Lynn Reynard again and after a short time he himself thought of her not at all.

Chapter 23.

JUDGE, LAWYER KILLED IN FREAK FALL, screamed the headline in the *Mohawk Valley Enterprise.*

DeWitt County Court Judge Samuel R. Blaine, 48, of Sanford Mills and Attorney Lynn Reynard, 29, of Bath Springs, who recently appeared in that court in the controversial Daisy Nichols murder trial, fell to their deaths Thursday in a freak accident from cliffs overlooking the Atlantic Ocean near Gold Harbor, Maine.

The two were in that resort community as part of a special retreat put together by Judge Blaine to ease the personal tensions caused by the three week trial and the judge's controversial decision to overturn the jury's verdict of Guilty and release Daisy Nichols from custody. Members of the DeWitt County Sheriff's Office, the District Attorney's Office as well as defense attorney Reynard had accepted the judge's invitation to spend a few days together in a neutral and relaxed setting at the popular summer resort town.

According to an eye witness, several of the party went for a nature walk near the dangerous cliffs just south of the famous beach in Gold Harbor. A sudden gust of wind knocked the slightly-built Ms. Reynard off balance and she began to fall. Judge Blaine, apparently with no consideration for his own safety, reached out to help her and tragically followed her over the edge. The pair plummeted nearly two hundred feet to their deaths.

DeWitt County Sheriff's Investigator Walter Heimlich, who witnessed the tragedy, was still in shock as he reported what he saw.

"It all happened so quickly," said Heimlich. "Everyone had been having a good time, relaxed and happy, then all of a sudden they're gone."

He added, "I tell you, what the Judge did was one of

-151-

the bravest things I've ever seen. We didn't always agree, but he was quite a guy."

Public officials and the community at large reacted in stunned disbelief to the news.

"He was a wonderful prosecutor and a fair judge," said Sheriff Emory Rushmore. "He will be sorely missed."

"I don't like this," said the District Attorney. "We set out to prove that Sam Blaine engaged in *ex parte* shenanigans during a murder trial, and we end up making a hero out of him. How does that help us in the Appellate Division?"

Sheriff Rushmore mused. "Well, with both of them dead, how would you ever prove anything? Yes, that reunion business raises the appearance of impropriety, but it doesn't prove a thing. For all we know, they never discussed the case at all. Besides, my friend, there is now a vacancy in the office of County Judge, and smearing the name of the dead incumbent is NOT the type of thing the governor would be likely to appreciate when he starts looking for a replacement."

"So I should just keep my mouth shut and let the case be decided on the record?"

"It would seem like a wise thing to do at this point."

The District Attorney shook his head. Then he shook his head again. Then he decided to be wise.

"Jack, I can't believe all the fun you have without me," said Maria as she sorted through the mail.

"Next time you can come with me," said Jack. "Although, frankly, I plan on staying away from Gold Harbor for a while."

"What was she like?"

"Who?"

"Lynn Reynard. Was she pretty?"

"Oh, I guess so, if you like that sort of thing."

"Did she go after you?"

"Me? Hey, I'm covered with the cloak of invincibility. Nobody can reach me as long as I'm married to the most wonderful woman in the world!" and he made a point of crossing the room to kiss her.

"So she did come after you."

"Yeah, well, maybe a little. But I won that round."

She looked worried. "Jack, promise me you'll always be strong."

"Always, darling, and you know why?"

"Why?"

"Because my strength comes from you."

-152-

It was the right answer.

"OK, here's your mail from Gold Harbor."

GOLD HARBOR NATIVE, FRIEND KILLED IN CLIFF FALL

Samuel R. Blaine, 48, a former resident of Gold Harbor, and his companion, Lynn Reynard of Bath Springs, New York fell to their deaths Thursday when a sudden gust of wind knocked them off the cliffs at the end of Gold Harbor Beach.

Ironically, although both were involved in the court system, Blaine as a judge in Upstate New York and Reynard as a defense attorney, the victims apparently ignored the warning signs posted by the Town Council and proceeded to the cliffs in violation of the Town Ordinances.

Members of the Town Council were already planning action.

"This ordinance has not been updated for thirty years," said Councilman Vito Rendrivino. I propose that we quadruple the fines to $200 effective immediately.

"Hey, Cuddy, do you know what they call it when a defense attorney and a judge fall off a cliff?"

"No, Alice, but I'm sure you'll tell me."

"A good start!" she cackled.

On March 23, 2000 the New York State Senate approved the Governor's appointment of the District Attorney as the new County Court Judge of DeWitt County. First Assistant District Attorney Tom Malcolm retired from the drudgery of night court in the ten towns to become Acting District Attorney and was himself confirmed in the position of District Attorney two months later. Jack Hughes was elevated to First Assistant.

Sheriff Rushmore reorganized his department with Bull Heimlich as Undersheriff in direct charge of all criminal investigations.

On the thirtieth of June the Appellate Division of the Supreme Court, Third Department, unanimously affirmed the decision of Judge Blaine dismissing the charges against Daisy Nichols. She was now officially free.

-153-

A t 3:45 a.m. on August 26, 2000 the phone rang.

"Jack, old buddy, what's happening?"

"Bull, do you only bother people in the middle of the night and on weekends?"

"Hey, never mind that, I got something for you. Get right up here." He gave him the address.

"I don't want to get in trouble with Tom."

"It's ok, I already cleared it with him. Really, I think you'll find this interesting."

Only once before had Jack Hughes seen this much blood.

Fortunately, this time there was no mayonnaise. And no strawberry jam.

There was, however, a body in a bloody heap on the living room floor. The coroner was making his arrangements while the Sheriff's technicians worked the scene.

"Jack, I'd like to introduce you to the late Mary Eckler Nichols. Her friends called her Polly," said Bull.

Polly. . .Eckler . . .Polly Eckler. Nichols.

"Not?"

"Yup. Daisy's mom. Now come with me." They stepped into the kitchen. "You remember Daisy, don't you, Jack?"

Daisy? This couldn't be Daisy Nichols. The woman seated at the table had soft, medium length blond hair, deep blue eyes, smooth face, long, professionally polished fingernails, a cute thirties retro outfit with a short-sleeved white top and ankle-length form-fitting blue skirt, something like Ginger Rogers might have worn, and suddenly Jack knew he had seen it before. Lynn Reynard had been wearing those same clothes the night of the felony hearing, the night when the CLANG CLANG CLANG brought him to his senses.

She was covered with blood, of course.

"Hello, Jack. I killed my mother," she spontaneously uttered.

"What say we all go for a ride to the office," suggested Bull.

"I got the idea from Lynn," she told them after being Mirandized. "She was always going how life is too short and you have to live for yourself and how it was important to confront the people who had abused you like she did with her brother. So I did."

"Yeah, but Daisy, I don't think Lynn Reynard *killed* her brother. Confronting's one thing, killing is something else," reasoned Bull.

"Oh, no, she killed him alright. Buried him herself."

"Well, ok, but how about we solve one case at a time. Tell us what

-154-

happened last night."

She had spent the afternoon in the beauty parlor. The contact lenses were a week old and gave her eyes that rich blue. She put on her snappiest clothes and matching shoes. She wanted to look her best for Mommy. She was delighted when her mother didn't recognize her.

"You see, Mommy, I didn't need you after all. I've done just fine without you."

"Underneath you're still the same useless piece of shit you always were," Mommy growled.

"I don't think so, *Mother*."

And now out came the knife, and she wanted a wound inflicted for every past hurt remembered, and she remembered many. She felt . . . detached, methodical, orderly. Once she began it was almost like doing piecework at the factory where she had worked most of her adult life. Couldn't remember whether Mother had said anything, or pleaded, or whined, or screamed. Daisy paid no attention to her whatsoever, and although it was over in a short time, she continued plunging the knife until a stiffness developed in her shoulder and only then decided it was enough. She carefully placed the knife by the body and washed her face and hands and arms in the bathroom. Proudly, she realized she had not broken a single nail.

She found her old bedroom and took a nap. When she woke up, she called the Sheriff's Office and patiently waited for them on the porch, her hands neatly folded across her blood-stained lap.

"Code 52?" asked Jack.

"Oh, yeah," said Bull.

Daisy Nichols would not be standing trial for a long time, if at all.

"So, Daisy, that's quite a story. So, tell me again, why did you do it?" asked Bull.

"I wanted to be like her."

"Like your mother?"

"No. Like *Lynn*."

What was that thing about the Bogeyman?

As long as she was being chatty, they decided to delve into the Patty Hartwick matter again. Jeopardy had attached, she could not be re-prosecuted, and because of her acquittal the investigation was still technically open.

It wasn't any one thing, but an endless series of annoyances that led Daisy to have that confrontation with Patty in the store. Patty was a little weird. Oh, they hung out together and worked together briefly, and a couple of times when they'd both been drinking and smoking dope they'd slept together, but it didn't mean anything. They weren't friends.

Daisy felt like she was close with Marge. Marge always talked to her before letting anyone rent one of the apartments. Daisy prided herself on her judgment.

What about Martin? Hey we all make a few mistakes.

Then Daisy finds out that Weird Patty is starting to get the hots for the landlady. *Hey, I don't know if Marge is like that, but I can't let Patty try it. Marge was* my *friend. Almost like a mother to me.*

So, every time Weird Patty brings this stuff up, Daisy keeps reminding her that she'd better shut up or I'll get you kicked out of here, and that night after they left the store, Patty goes upstairs and starts making noises and when Daisy tells her to cut it out she starts saying stuff like "Marge loves Patty, Marge loves Patty in a nauseating sing-song, so first Daisy goes upstairs and throws those two jars against the door, and still she won't shut up, so now Martin can't stand it either, so he gets a screwdriver and the two of them take turns trying to figure out how to open the door and finally Daisy gets it to pop off in her hands and now she's really mad and POW to the side of her head and finally the little bitch shuts up, but then she starts whimpering and telling her it's not Marge she wants but Daisy and that's it for Daisy who takes out her knife and says, "Get away from me, you weirdo" and slashes her and Patty throws the beer bottle at her and how could she say such a thing in front of Martin especially, and now Daisy is all hot and storms out of there.

She walks over to Marie's house and tells her some of it, but now she starts worrying and figures she'd better make amends with Patty before she calls the cops and gets her in trouble, so she goes back to her apartment and asshole Martin is sleeping on her couch, so she goes upstairs to see Patty and she's in her chair in the living room and there's Marge right there with her.

Marge? Yeah, Marge Brown, sitting right next to her and holding her and making all these soft noises and stroking her hair and saying, "It's ok, Patty, it's ok."

And then she sees Daisy and she stands up and says, "Daisy Nichols, what you did here is bad. Very bad. You are one bad girl."

And now Daisy is suddenly afraid she will be punished and no, not again, I'm not taking any more of this, not now, not never and she looks at Marge Brown and all she can see is Mommy and the big board and the stove and the shivering cold and the searing flesh and the cigarettes and the alcohol on her

-156-

breath and that hand slapping, slapping and fists beating, beating, beating, and no one is protecting her from Daddy, where was Mommy then? And she goes into a rage and she takes out the knife and charges Marge and Marge somehow holds her off and they start struggling and she just wants to KILL HER, KILL HER and she breaks her arm loose and pulls the knife over her head and brings it down hard on Marge.

Only Marge has moved and the knife keeps on going right through Patty Hartwick and Daisy doesn't even know the difference, she's blinded with all those bad feelings and keeps on sticking that knife until she realizes what she has done and steps back in horror.

Marge tells her now do what I tell you, Daisy. Do what I tell you. We've got to get out of here and you must never tell anyone you saw me and I'll help you. And they forget all about Patty sitting in the chair bleeding to death and they quick make sure there is nothing there to lead to Marge and they go into the bathroom to wash off the knife and all of a sudden Patty stumbles behind them and out the door and they run to catch up, but Patty's already down the stairs and now Martin is awake so Marge steps back inside Patty's apartment and while Martin is following Patty, Daisy hides the knife under her mattress and runs back out and closes the door behind her and only then remembers that she's locked herself out and can't get back in for the knife unless she goes out on the roof and there's no time for that, she just wants to get the hell out of there so she and Martin push Patty aside to get to the street and then they finally stop and start to think. Martin tells her he left the chicken on the stove, 'cause he fell asleep while he was pre-heating the oven. She sends Martin off hopping in one direction, because she doesn't want him to know about Marge because Marge told her not to, and then she sees Marge go out the window and over the porch and down by the garage. She must have got into her car and gone home, 'cause that's where she was later.

Then Martin comes back and thinks he hears something in the alley so he goes to check while Daisy goes next door for help. Later, when she jumps out of the ambulance she runs to Marge's house and says she doesn't know what to do, so Marge tells her exactly what to say and what not to say and says she'll take care of the rest of the family. And she does.

"Marge was a very good mommy, Bull. I should have had a mommy like her."

Jack needed some air. "Bring Ms. Nichols a coffee," he hollered to a deputy in the next room. "And a doughnut. Bring her the biggest strawberry-filled jelly doughnut you can find."

Bull and Jack sat on the bench outside the front door of the Sheriff's Office for a long time without saying a word. Every once in a while they'd look at each other, shake their heads and go back to nothing. Finally Bull broke the silence.

"You're just a tiny little bit curious, aren't you?"

"About what?"

"You know. Lynn and the brother."

Jack sighed. "Won't she ever just go away? Yeah, I guess I am just a tiny little bit curious."

"It was like this," sparkled Daisy as she wiped some strawberry filling off her chin, "she goes 'You don't have to tolerate your abuse. Face it head on like I did.'"

It was twenty years ago after a huge snowstorm that had left the Reynard house isolated from the world way out in the country. All the roads were closed for miles, school canceled, and the wintery wonderland just an enchanting place for the Reynard children to play in. There were five of them now, dashing off in all directions. All except Lynn, sitting alone in her room, the room where her brother kept bothering her every time her parents went out.

She was tired of getting hurt down there and the way her brother nearly smothered her every time when he was on top and doing those things. She was getting really mad, but she knew he was Momma's favorite, her first-born and light of her life.

She looked out the window, past the edge of the porch roof, and saw him playing with her younger sister, saw him tickle her and run after her and wrestle with her in the snow, saw her giggling and laughing.

It had been a long winter. Big chunks of ice lay under the new snow on that roof. She was little, but she was strong, strong enough to throw open the window and climb out. Strong enough to brace her little feet against one of those blocks of ice with her back pressed against the wall. Strong enough to push and set the ice in motion slowly, slowly toward the edge when she knew he would be coming by. She saw it slip over, heard the crash, heard her sister scream.

No one saw.

There were no telephones working, no roads open. It was nearly four hours before help arrived, and by then he was nearly dead, the whole left side of his head smashed in.

He remained in a coma for nearly three months, and when he finally began to recover, his speech was slurred, he had trouble walking, his right arm was useless, and he was unable to learn very much in school.

He never bothered her again.

But the brother, he got all the attention. Momma quit work to stay home with him, waited on him twenty-four hours a day while the others learned to fend for themselves. It made Lynn very angry and as she got older the resentment built and built.

When at last they were adults, they avoided each other, until their mother's final illness brought them together again at the old homestead. "Take care of your brother," Momma whispered to her at the end.

Lynn had by this time been through a failed marriage and numerous transient and unhealthy relationships. She read a lot of books, and had a pretty good grasp of the reason. So after the funeral, when it was just her and the brother, she confronted him with all her years of pent-up rage, all screaming and aquivering, her face transformed from beauty to barbarity. He walked away. She followed. He went into the old barn, tried to close the door behind him, but she flung it open. With his handicap he was no match for her, and could barely raise an arm to protect himself from the shovel as it came crashing down on his head, over and over and over.

She buried him where he fell.

"So that's it, guys," said Daisy. "You understand, right?"

"You understand, don't you, Jack old buddy?" Bull laughed as the car pulled away to take Daisy to the Psychiatric Ward of the local hospital. "It all makes sense, right?"

"Bull," said Jack slowly, "I once saw Lynn Reynard as an attractive, friendly, confident, talented attorney. Then I saw her as a cold, calculating, dangerous woman. And now . . . now it looks like the cover was nothing, that, underneath, all that ever existed, I guess, was a pretty little seven year old girl repeatedly molested, repeatedly . . . *diminished* by a member of her own family. And you know what, Bull? No one ever jumped in to stop her diminishing, not ever. She must have borne the scars of that experience her entire life and I'll bet it affected every relationship that she was ever in, and that the reason she fell in love over and over and over again was because she found . . . . she found, I think, that maybe only the thrill of new love is strong enough to overcome the pain of lost innocence and that even her killing her brother was just another way of striking back at that pain that would never leave her. That's what I think."

He looked to Bull for concurrence. He waited.

"You're feeling all mushy-sympathetic toward Lynn, now, right?"

"After all that happened to her? Come on. Of course."

"Yeah, well, there's always another possibility," said Bull.

"What's that?"

"Maybe Lynn made the whole thing up. You know, just to set things in motion and see what would happen."

Jack was shocked. "No one is that evil."

Bull raised an eyebrow. "Think about it. Lynn was pretty smart, right?"

"Absolutely."

"And a good lawyer?"

"Without a doubt."

"In a million years would a good, smart lawyer admit to one of her dirt-bag clients that she had murdered someone, then tell her where the body was buried?"

Jack frowned. "Not likely, I suppose. But still . . ."

"One more thing, Jack. I forgot to tell you."

"What's that?" asked Jack as they slowly moved toward their cars.

Bull waited until he was ready to drive off.

"I talked to her brother, day before yesterday."

"What?"

"Yeah, he's kinda weird, like they said. He's been bumming around the country last few years and just found out Lynn was dead. He wanted to know what happened."

Jack stared at him.

"I think. . . I think . . . I think I need a beer," he said.

Bull laughed uproariously. "Jack, it's only eight in the morning!"

"Who makes these rules?"

Epilogue

On a fine September day Jack Hughes and his young family arrived in Glasgow, Scotland. There was someone Jack wanted to see there, but he found she had died several years earlier.

So they rented a car and drove to Loch Lomonde and inquired about hiring a boat for the afternoon.

"Is it a motor boat you'll be wanting?"

"No, sir. A rowboat if you have one."

And so he took his lovely wife and his lovely children for a lovely ride on a lovely day. And when they had reached a certain spot where the autumn colors and the afternoon sun and the sparkling waters were as close to perfect as God could have intended, Jack Hughes pulled a small box from his pocket.

He removed the item, kissed it, swung the chain three times around his head and released.

Then they watched in reverential silence as the World War II dog tags of Francis J. Hughes gently merged with the bonnie blue waters of Loch Lomonde.

The End

Acknowledgments

Special thanks to Montgomery County, NY Surrogate Judge Guy P. Tomlinson for his many helpful suggestions concerning the legal issues in this novel, his inspiration as a former Assistant District Attorney and District Attorney, and his encouragement and friendship.

Many thanks also to present and former law enforcement personnel, particularly retired Sgt. William Pedrick and Detective Walter Boice of the Amsterdam, NY Police Department, the late Investigator Jim Hutchison and the late Deputy Gary Johnson of the Montgomery County Sheriff's Office, all of whose actual exploits far exceed those of any fictional characters, and all of whom brought honor to their profession.

Deep appreciation and thanks to my friends who have read various drafts of this work and offered helpful suggestions and mostly appropriate criticism, including Carol Dillon, Ellen Ross, Nora Krupczak, Marie Wiley, the late great Bill Lamphere, Becky Gomula, Dan Blanchfield (but not his brother Tim who never got around to reading it) and my brother Sean T. Going.

To my sister Dale, the genuine poet in the family, I apologize for making the poems rhyme.

Kudos to Dee Dee Bubniak, Mary Grace Sullivan, Donna Soper, Donna Ross, Sarah Craig, Marsha Prokop and Donna Phelps for bringing sunshine to the Montgomery County Family Court.

To Mary and our children, Anna, Bob, Jamie and Louisa, and my sweet granddaughter Laura Ann, no thanks could ever be enough, and my love for you is endless.

-RNG

Made in the USA